No Safewords
A Marketplace Fan Anthology

edited by Laura Antoniou

Luster Editions

Circlet Press, Inc.
Cambridge, MA

Also by Laura Antoniou

Marketplace Novels & Story Collections:
The Marketplace
The Slave
The Trainer
The Academy
The Reunion
The Inheritor (forthcoming)
Slaves of the Marketplace (forthcoming)

Marketplace Digital Short Stories:
For Want of a Nail
That's Harsh
California Dreaming
Inside Straight
Ollie's Present

Contents

7   Introduction

14   A Thousand Things Before Breakfast
by Marie Casey Stevens

24   The First
by D. Alexandria

42   If You Try Sometime
by D. L. King

53   Her Owner's Voice
by Leigh Ann Hildebrand

75   Hiding in Plain Sex
by Sassafras Lowrey

86   Delirious Moonlight, 1916: Mr. Sloan's Boy
by Anna Watson

105   Pearls in the Deep Blue Sea
by Jamie Thorsen

126   Coals for the New Castle
by Marie Casey Stevens

151   Getting Real
by S. M. Li

163   O, Promise Me!
by Elizabeth Schechter

Introduction

I've always written fan fiction. This is actually news to me. But as I was pondering the introduction to this collection, my first thought was to explain how I was always suspicious of fan fiction, despite enjoying it from time to time.

(Especially smutty *Star Trek* stories. I have actual printed fanzines from the 70s in my home library. You may covet my copies of *The Sensuous Vulcan* now.)

But a funny thing happened on the way to this introduction. Somewhere along the brain path where I was building an orderly and brief description of the stories, a standard "here's the stuff!" sort of thing, I slowly realized that my first creative writing was completely based in fictional worlds someone else developed.

And I'm not talking about The Marketplace—although I will, shortly. I mean the stories I wrote as a child.

The first influence I remember was a Scholastic book titled *Greek Slave Boy*, by Lillian Carroll. It was published in 1968 and no doubt I got it from one of those catalogs they would distribute in schools from time to time. I'd check off as many books as I thought I could get away with and come into class one day to find them stacked on my desk like treasure.

Reading this one, however, was quite the breakthrough moment for me. I instantly knew I was not supposed to have the thoughts I was having upon reading such a story. I was not supposed to want to know more about this whole slavery thing. I should not feel thrilled by the aspect of selling children.

Or, tying them up and whipping them. Oh, yeah. This book had stuff I would not be allowed to depict in my books for adults, but I was reading it around age 7 or 8! It's enough to make you laugh.

Eventually, I re-read it so many times I memorized some parts.

This was clearly not acceptable, so for the first time, I wrote down my own version of what might happen to a young Greek slave boy. I hid them, pulling them out to read by flashlight at night, or tucked among the piles of text and notebooks on my bed. Eventually, I tore them into tiny scraps and threw them away. I didn't want anyone to find them.

Later on, I wrote stories about a female descendant of Van Helsing, fighting Dracula and assorted other vampires in modern day London. She had a gay BFF and taught history and hunted bloodsuckers on the side. This was fan fiction not only of *Dracula*, by Bram Stoker, but *Tomb of Dracula*, the Marvel comic book lavishly illustrated by the amazing Gene Colon, with a little bit of Hammer film fangirl love tossed in there for good measure.

Multi-media fan fiction!

And then there was my huge fantasy novel about people questing for a magical talisman. Yeah, nothing too original there, either, except for a lot of frustrated sexual longing. But I was a teenager, so anything I wrote was going to be shot through with frustrated sexual longing.

And then there's the Marketplace.

Some people think I based the Marketplace on Anne Rice's *Exit to Eden*. This is not so. Rice's book did show the sale of consensual slaves with some sort of rudimentary training, but it was very small and limited and let's have a moment of honesty here. A chief trainer who lets a brand new slave get away with calling her "cutie" and then proceeds to be seduced into running away with him is not exactly a role model for a working system. Exit to Eden was, in a way, an example of a story that should have worked for me, but didn't at all.

The real inspiration for the Marketplace series was John Preston's books about The Network—*I Once Had a Master, Entertainment For a Master*, and mostly, *The Love of a Master*. Preston imagined a worldwide secret society of loosely organized trainers and private auctions, and of course, a never-ending array of increasingly gorgeous, muscular, well hung young men to kneel on his mirror-topped tables.

That was more like it.

I read them until I had to buy replacement copies. I took one, stammering my admiration, to ask Preston to sign it. And then, later on, I told him I was writing my own version of that huge secret slave training and selling society, only mine would have all sorts of people in it, not just gay men. And he gave me some excellent advice and told me he had often wished he could have written exactly that.

He died before I could find out what he thought of what I did. But I think of him often when I write—especially when I write about handsome, hunky, well-hung young gay men. The Marketplace short story, "Brian on the Farm", which I wrote for the collection *Switch Hitters*, edited by Carol Queen and Lawrence Schimel, was written specifically with Preston in mind.

Tributary fan fiction.

Yet, despite what seems obvious now, I maintained a stubborn resistance to the idea of sharing my world with other writers. I was a victim of a paranoid fear of intellectual property theft mingled with a hyperactive protectiveness of my special little snowflake of a world. Even when I decided to open the Marketplace to other writers, it was by invitation only, for *The Academy*. Originally, I had intended *The Academy* to be an anthology, but instead wound up creating a hybrid book I called a novelogy— a novel with stories framed by the device of being oral tales shared by various characters. The authors I invited were all trusted friends who wouldn't run off and immediately publish—and sell!— knockoffs of my precious world.

The hubris and vigilance seem kind of funny now.

So what changed? My resistance wavered with *The Academy*, but took a deep body blow with the creation of the online Marketplace role-playing game.

This was the brainchild of my dear friend and lifestyle co-conspirator, Kim Attica. (Oh, hai, Daddy!) She idly asked me one day if I would mind the creation of such a text/chat based game. She already hosted hundreds of users on a talker—an online community called Iron Rose. There, she indexed articles and interviews about SM, leather, and the dominant/submissive paradigm, plus live chatting channels set up with themes to accommodate everyone from the complete novice to the heavily invested multi-user-dungeon veteran to actual kinky people who just liked to connect with their buddies online. Much of this was pretty cutting edge for the time.

She asked, coincidentally, at a time when I was feeling a certain sense of disconnection with my readers. People imagine I get tons of fan mail and praise and feedback. The truth is, I often feel like I am writing in front of a giant turbine. I finish and let the pages go and they scatter away without any way of my knowing what people think about them. Reviews? We in the erotica market are lucky if we get a few of our friends to post nice things on a major booksellers website.

And I am a mass of insecurities wrapped up in ego. (See: definition of "writer.") I wanted, desperately, to hear people talk about my books. To know what they thought. So, I said, sure, make the game. I figured I would learn how to use this talker thing and maybe peek in once in a while to see what people were doing there.

Quicksand couldn't have sucked me in any better. Within hours of its creation, I made up a hunky gay bartender character, thinking (rightly) that eventually, most characters would investigate the "leather bar" chat room and I could eavesdrop on their storytelling.

Yeah. That lasted a few minutes. Soon, I was playing along, creating multiple characters and getting invested in story lines, role-playing; all the good stuff. I made friends. I outed myself. (Sometimes by accident.) There was drama, and laughter and angst and weirdness. And my life was changed. But more to the point, my attitude about other people in my playground changed. I can't thank Kim Attica enough for the Marketplace RPG and the amazing things that came out of it. I am no longer the paranoid writer clutching my words to my heart with terror in my eyes. But I am still desperately curious about what my readers think. Now, I want to hear their stories. Because they are not taking anything from my creation—they are adding to it.

Sadly, this realization first came at a time when my books were going out of print. But with my new publisher and the ease of marketing e-books, I can open the gates to people just like me. People who show how much they like a world by playing in it, thinking about it, embellishing it.

And as the saying goes, "blessed are those who embellish the tale."

So here is the Marketplace, as seen through other eyes. There are some stories that show the world exactly as I created it, and some that push my boundaries a tad. They are short and sweet, which makes a story unlike what I usually write, or long and involved. There is romance and strife, glee and despair. There is hot sex, of course, but there's also humor and melodrama. Just the way I like it.

There were some surprises for me! I was delighted to find several female dominant/male submissive stories, especially since my examples of those relationships tend to be supporting, rather than main characters. I was also pleased by the writers who weren't afraid to go a little dark; a collection of stories all about slaves misbehaving in mildly inconvenient ways and getting fantastically, erotically punished would have been tiresome.

So whether you want a rollicking Victorian flavored tale of adventure and romance or a modern, sexy welcome to a new home for a familiar character, you will find flavors here to tempt or satisfy your tastes. Return for more time travel to a world where the language we so casually use to describe our tastes doesn't even exist, but where longing for a ritualized order and discipline and a sense of belonging transcends words, and gets expressed in the rich metaphor—and reality—of a garden.

Then swerve away from romance to feel the terror of a slave newly sold to an owner who represents their worst nightmare, whether because of demographics or the enormous challenge of a language barrier.

Here, you can get into the reflection of a trainer's long career or the grief and anguish of a new owner confronted with an inherited house full of property she didn't choose. Or, watch how even the jaded, experienced ways of the Marketplace aware people become awkward in that most awkward of adult challenges—a marriage proposal.

Get a glimpse into the rarefied and formal household of an owner/spotter, and then take a detour to the desolate history of a young genderqueer punk fresh from the streets, confronted with the most iconic of Marketplace characters.

All of this—a synthesis of my imagination and theirs, fed by culture, fantasy, fairy tales and fears. All fiction is, in a way, fan fiction. I am sorry it took so long for me to see this and to open myself to the interesting sensations—you might call it edge-play—in giving people access to my favorite victims. But better late than never!

It was hard to choose stories for this collection. There were some I lingered over, and a few I wish I had the freedom to publish. (But some subjects remain taboo even for the kinkiest of erotica publishers.) The authors I chose range from old hands at this sort of thing to brand new postulants to the rude gods of publishing, as it should be. I hope your journey through these tales whets your appetite for more stories in this world and others, and maybe even sparks a desire to tell a story of your own. I am already thinking of doing this again, hoping to get more lesbian stories, more stories of trans and genderqueer people, more stories told from the perspective of owners. And yes, maybe even a paranormal or futuristic story, because this is Circlet Press, after all. In the meantime, I will continue to work on my other books, in and out of the Marketplace, to make the playground even bigger. I hope there's plenty of room for you to romp!

Laura Antoniou
September 2012

Foreword

The first time I opened the Marketplace to other authors was for *The Academy*, in which I invited some talented folks to contribute cautionary tales the various trainers and spotters told each other at their annual gathering. Of course, I had in mind the many kinky/leather/BDSM conferences held throughout the world when I designed my Okinawan retreat, complete with formal sessions, bylaws, performance art, contests, interpersonal and political dramas, hooking up and general orgies. What I left out was... a speech. Having given more than my share, I was glad to see Marie Casey Stevens stepped up to correct my egregious exclusion. This will not be her only appearance in this collection, because when I find someone who plays nicely in my dungeon, I like to invite them back.

Marie Casey Stevens' only redeeming qualities are the people who care about her. Marie's parents Janice and Charles Stevens encouraged her to be herself... regardless of how that turned out. Janet Casey listened to everything... and that's saying something. Ms. Vukelich provides the five Stevens cats and single Stevens human with multiple forms of sustenance, and Robin Warninghoff helps make her house a home from many states away. Andrew Warninghoff makes sure that home—and many others—stays safe. Amanda Wilkes keeps her spine straight, her caffeine addiction fed, and her feet shod in delicious boots. Kathy and Cary LeBrasseur gave her understanding and the wheels to do what needed to be done. J LeBrasseur does complicated things for a complicated person in a way that's indescribably... complicated.

Marie just writes fiction and tries her best to be of use to these people and others in a way that makes them proud.

A Thousand Things Before Breakfast
Marie Casey Stevens

[Transcription of speech presented before The Academy on November 11th, 20—by Ms. Jorgean Kasden]

Good evening, ladies and gentlemen. As some of you know, my name is Jorgean P. Kasden. Before I proceed, is everyone comfortable?

[Laughter]

Of course not. Permit me to ask the correct question. Is everyone content?

[Chuckles, muted applause]

Over the years I have had the honor and privilege of presenting papers on points of methodology in service, training, and ownership. My contributions have focused on the ideal use of linguistics in the various roles of The Marketplace. In "The Semantics of Service" I addressed advanced communication skills both within and beyond voice training for slaves. "Slaves to Linguistics" examined the unique demands of vocabulary required for second and third language education of slaves. "Tongue Lashings: The Art of Commanding Communication" provided a primer for both owners and trainers in diction specifically suited to both roles. Articulation has been the expression of my service to the Academy.

We in the Marketplace are frequently creatures of dates and anniversaries, for reasons I shall elaborate on. Approaching my thirtieth year as a part of this institution in one capacity or another, I have given much thought to two questions pondered throughout those three decades. What am I doing here, and what are we doing here?

Everyone here knows the infinite tones of the former question. Before the heating, beating, and eating come scores of exasperated moments regardless of one's place. A slave asks the question when confronted with the most repellant mundane task imaginable. A trainer hears it when paralyzing headache encroaches but the task at hand demands work rather than respite. Owners have been known to think it from time to time when care for and of property manifests itself as a cost ranging from the ridiculous and amusing to the uncomfortable and expensive. The thousand things before the breakfast of best bits have made each of us ask ourselves "What am I doing here" in voices from bewildered to hostile... even if restrained to vehement mutters.

We find that answer in those breakfasts, those times when we break our fasts with the moments we came here for. We ask ourselves the question again, with wonder and awe. What am I doing here? What did I do to get this moment, this life? Our contentment and gratitude nearly defy articulation.

What are we doing here? The philosophers among us have asked themselves this question. What is the purpose of the Marketplace? We have asked each other privately and listened to the answers we get carefully because few questions remain so personal and private to us. To answer smacks of hubris.

I offer my answer, humbly, as my gift to this institution for the thirty years it has given me.

The spotter asks, "What am I doing here?" Blended moonshine masquerades as top shelf scotch, mood lighting doesn't make for a good mood and the only slaves are the slaves to fashion. The local fauna? Greedy bottoms too incorrigible to benefit from the correction they don't deserve, prancing around on leashes held by laissez-faire "masters" and "mistresses" as teeth-grittingly irritating as oblivious parents ignoring riotous children at the grocery store. The flora? Save us from the dueling colognes and perfumes. Please.

The worst bartender in the place possesses better talent for service than anyone present in or hoping for a collar, and at home there's beauty and all the punishment of a much anticipated taped episode of Top Chef Masters waiting with a properly presented single malt.

Why does the spotter spot? When does "What am I doing

here" become a spotter's most heartfelt expression of gratitude for this life, and awe at the miracle of being the one to have it? When it comes together, when the spotter's purpose and the fulfillment of it join and function in an act of beauty that so often go unrecognized.

The spotter exists as a witness, recognizing special characteristics in people who could otherwise spend a lifetime in a life other than the one they were meant for. Spotters hone their own talent, the ability to see a rare combination of talent and calling in others. Then they perform a staggering act of charity: they bring people to the opportunity to earn the place most likely to let them find and share the very best of themselves in a world only equipped to provide poor substitutes of that existence. To those who benefit from the spotter's work, fees alone cannot compensate anyone for such munificence.

The spotter serves beauty and harmony: the beauty of a potential slave's true calling to service, the beauty of a potential owner's development of talent, and the plenary perfection of harmony when the two find their way to each other. Lives are changed for the better, and an improved world spins a fraction more satisfactorily on its axis every time it happens.

My favorite instance of a trainer voicing the words "What am I doing here?" occurred a few days ago. Romantic ideas, abject terror, and awe from trainees aside, we all know trainers have personal problems like everyone else. One trainer, a dear friend of mine in collared service, had a particularly traumatic morning. Her trainees had failed to clean the shower room properly, leaving both a detachable shower head handle and a crucial piece of the large room's tile floor slippery. A small mishap ensued involving very personal grooming, a razor blade improperly stored, and slippery surfaces. This put my friend in a truly foul humor the morning of my arrival.

While chastising them, she used the word "froward" in particular to one pupil working on mastering inappropriate verbal impulses. The trainee reverted to form with a mistaken attempt at correction, saying, "You mean I'm terminally forward?"

[Laughter]

I had the pleasure of arriving to find my friend, uncharacteristically disheveled and sitting uncomfortably while her trainee wrote "habitually disposed to disobedience and opposition" in tiny grease pencil letters covering the shower room—which of course he then had to clean to perfection. His trainer certainly wanted to repair to her room with a nice analgesic cream rather than ensure the lesson finally penetrated the trainee's grey matter. This promoted her barely audible "What am I doing here?" She remained to supervise, however. Why?

For those moments when what she was doing produced that which she was meant to do. Her calling to teach, to impart wisdom, manifested itself even in that moment in a way no underfunded school district full of mother's little darlings could have brought to full fruition. The area she hailed from would have chewed up the charity of her sincere vocation and fed it back to her in the form of near poverty, constant legal hostility from lazy over-empowered children and unconscionably poor medical care, spitting her out exhausted at a young age as "too old to continue her service."

Like many, she desires a legacy. Not all offspring oblige in providing one to be proud of, though, and in her case that wasn't an option. That did not diminish her desire to leave this world with someone of her, a human being of substance, wisdom, education, and kindness, in this world after her service in it ends.

I know for a fact that she whispers "Why am I here?" every time a trainee of hers goes on the block, and after every single time she encounters a former trainee happy in his or her service. While perhaps more demonstrative than many of her peers with this ritual of sentimentality—she would credit her Irish heritage— she expresses what all of her best peers have felt: wonder. She marvels every time that she was so exquisitely fortunate as to touch this life, and that one, and the next, to both help her trainees find their best selves and have the privilege of seeing them succeed.

For each froward moment, the others answer the question of why she is here.

Of course the owners have the purview to say for themselves what motivates their participation in the Marketplace, but in present company I submit my own answer. It will differ significantly from the "heating, beating, eating, and cleaning" answers assumed by the ignorant or who given by those who deflect a serious question too close for comfort.

Becoming an owner of a Marketplace slave is not the easiest way to have a desire for any service needs met. Any employee outside the Marketplace might cost less. Without exception, any employee would require less care, maintenance, and commitment.

However, it is that last which proves essential. Owners possess a commitment to an ideal of service which, through their owner-ship, they provide patronage for. Explicitly and consciously or not, they complete the equation of service by virtue of the validation, appreciation, and proof of purpose inherent in their act of ownership.

An artist can find a degree of satisfaction and fulfillment in a finished work; many couldn't care less whether their pieces find homes let alone public acclaim. On the other hand, while a slave truly dedicated to service requires no praise for a successfully completed task, that task must serve someone else. That is the nature of the calling. Some slaves can only find satisfaction in tasks performed for others. The existence of owners validates this character trait as a noble and worthwhile quality in a world that increasingly lauds narcissism over humility, and fame over the quiet but passionate pursuit of perfection without tangible personal gain. The owner's want legitimizes the slave's need, demonstrates indisputably the appreciative value of the calling or desire to serve, and proves with purchase that the slave's purpose has the dignity of merit.

Some would also point out their financial contribution to the Marketplace certainly helps.

[Laughter]

And of course, many wonder why slaves are here. Many owners

find the notion of service entirely foreign to the point of incomprehensibility. I'd wager that naughty froward trainee wondered why he continued to pursue his "dream" when it included remedial English in the form of bathroom graffiti followed by janitorial duties. The tedious, the irritating, and the discomfiting moments make us all forwardly ask, if only once, "What am I doing here?" in tones as far removed from reverie as imaginable.

A year and a half ago, I conducted the interview process of a slave preparing to enter a lifetime contract with her owner of seven years. The previous contracts had been for one, two, and five years. While many of her daily functions were of no enjoyment to her as a matter of personal preference, her sense of contentment permeated the air around her. Laughing, she expressed the most charming wonder that even properly making the bed gave her joy. This woman who considered making the bed for herself as pointless and futile as shoreline sand castles simply could not get over her wonder at being the person granted a life where even that mundane task could give her joy. What was she, an ordinary person who could have wound up in any other circumstances, doing there, in such a life?

Slaves complete their part of the equation; their existence providing the art which spotters need to seek, the commitment trainers are called to sculpt and the combination of trust and service owners seek to achieve perfection. They are the spotters' charity, the trainers' legacy and the owners' artists.

Together, all form the totality upon which the Marketplace is built.

Why is the Marketplace here?

We here this evening have a more intimate knowledge than most of the Marketplace's mundane functions. An entity must exist to manage matters related to what we all do that its external counterparts either cannot or will not. Contracts must be drafted, witnessed, archived, and enforced. Someone must oversee the economics of purchases, remunerations, and other fiscal matters.

A postulant in any faith desires spiritual immersion. For every meditating being in a moment of reverie, other eyes lift upwards—after frequent glances down at bills for water, sewer, and electricity. For every artist struggling for perfection, thousands of hands produce pigments, clays, instruments, and other supplies. The Marketplace does this.

It answers the mundane knock at the door of our world so we may practice our calling. By dint of its commitment and consistency it protects us, regardless of our role within it, from exploitation. It provides the support needed for us to strive for the sublime.

The Marketplace staff has its share of existential professional angst, to be sure. Much as we wish it were so, not all members of an institution meet its standards. The more extreme failures in every role from spotter to slave cause as much dismay to those in what can seem to us a detached and nebulous group as they do to us.

They do not go to work every day yearning to impose sanctions and bans. They don't rush through their morning grooming eager to file a contract in three locations or move payments for property and training. That's what they do, but why are they here? For what, all that elbow grease?

The ends sanctify the elbow grease.

Let justification sit with the protesters outside where it belongs, with old news. We don't need to justify our existence. We deserve to breathe, to strive for personal improvement, to exist. We even deserve for our struggle to transcend a merely justifiable and acceptable existence to attain a sublime one, a life in which one's actions from waking to sleeping reflect our highest ideals and aspirations. Like the name of the art dealer who sold the painting that kept Degas in pigments, like the church or temple secretary crunching the numbers to make transportation for clergy calls to hospice patients possible, the functionaries of the Marketplace do two things. They do away with justification and provide each of us our very own blank Sistine Chapel ceiling. Then, they give us a chance to defy the probable outcome of personal mediocrity by believing in and expecting the extraordinary from us.

A spotter sees a riveting example of humanity: sincere, determined, and inimitable. Buried under layers of dust and debris almost every time, this work of art appears displayed improperly. The lighting diminishes it, frames fail to flatter, and other pieces nearby obscure it to everyone else. Its future follows a path of probable outcomes from this moment to the human equivalent of a poorly framed and unsigned thrift store painting that will merely occupy space above a sofa.

The Marketplace provides the pedestal, the lighting, and the acoustics that let what the spotter witnesses stand, shine, and be heard properly. Not in dusty attics, indifferently displayed, or as the aria needed by the world but only sung in the interior of a car on the solitary drive home from work. The Marketplace gives the spotter the very gift he or she bestows upon others: a worthy destination.

To so many, service is a dead language. Outside these walls, it always refers to something or someone other than the speaker. "Good service" is expected at restaurants and businesses and from others. Entities—businesses, hospitals—promise or voice commitment to excellent service that other people, the employees, will deliver. To say one wishes to serve is to provoke cynical suspicion in the manner of a politician lauding commitment to "public service," or admitting a sort of social abnormality in the manner of an aspiring nun or priest. To aspire to perfect not fame, protagonism, glory, or accolades is a reference as dead as "me and thee". Beyond these walls, to teach it and to study it is seems as senseless a life where one immersed in Latin or ancient Greek.

To the trainers, the Marketplace gives a specialized Coliseum. The language of service not only lives and breathes but also grows and evolves. It makes gladiators of us all as we fight our own cowardice and imperfections and debate amongst ourselves. The skills we teach find glory on the sand of the auction block and our own arenas of service: our students, savoring the sun on their shoulders as they take their proper place, put marrow in our very bones.

It gives us a Bayt Ul-Hikma, a House of Wisdom that we may learn from; and one we may contribute to. With this, we may build a legacy beyond our own existences. Regardless of societal disapproval and ignorance, these scrolls of our hard-won education will remain, cared for by the Marketplace in the face of any challenge.

Owners and slaves receive two sides of the same coin from this institution. Both find an environment where their dispositions are prized rather than scorned, and where these dispositions can find harmony rather than rejection. Both can enter a system of artistic patronage within the Marketplace.

The Marketplace permits slaves to be the art they are rather than abide in roles designed by societies who hold nothing but contempt for the quiet, the unassuming, the earnest, and the sincere. A blessed percentage find a means for their simple need to be of use, where their worth is reckoned at true value rather than exploited or taken for granted. That place also does not come with an expiration date determined by mandatory retirement dates. The Marketplace provides equal opportunity employment in its truest form: the most experienced among us are treasured.

The Marketplace exists to serve service itself, to ensure this quality is not only preserved but also promoted. Vagaries of trend and popular culture will sway from the "me generation" to the "all about me" generation, political phases will emerge and pass; this is true. Fostering both the spirit of service and its practitioners in safety, however, is the calling the staff of the Marketplace answers to.

I thank you for inviting me to speak, and for listening to me this evening. Please feel free to disagree with my conclusions. I've been known to require correction in the past... and to have even welcomed it.

[Laughter]

To those who have helped me form these conclusions through your examples, thank you. We are creatures of dates and anniversaries, contracts and commitment. Nothing pleases me more than having been able to share my coming anniversary with you.

[Sustained applause]

Foreword

From the self-congratulatory keynote speech where everyone in the Marketplace is a hero, I will shift into a story perhaps a little more frightening. One of the biggest reasons why the Marketplace is fiction is not that it can't exist as a giant secret organization. Fiction is full of giant, secret organizations and we can accept that in order to move on to the thrilling adventures of super spies, vampires, time travelers, and political paranoia. The biggest "lie" of the Marketplace is that there would be so many people willing to enter it as slaves. While a robust fantasy, well sustained in the kinky subculture and celebrated endlessly, most sane adults actually have some very serious preferences and limitations that would prevent them from just happily going off with anyone clutching the price of a contract, no matter how generous. So, I was thrilled to accept two stories depicting slaves who experience the sheer terror of discovering that life in such a world will not always deliver the fantasy owner of their dreams. Indeed, it might seem like their worst fears have coalesced in the moment of a lock being secured. In this sexy tale, an experienced slave realizes her luck in avoiding her worst-case scenario—until it finally happens.

Boston native D. Alexandria is the author of the Lambda Literary Award finalist *This Is How We Do It: A Raw Mix of Lesbian Erotica*. Her work has appeared in the *Best Lesbian Erotica* series (2005-2009), *Sometimes She Lets Me: Best Butch Femme Erotica*, *Ultimate Lesbian Erotica 2006*, and at Kuma2.net

The First
D. Alexandria

Three significant things happened to Davina Warren during the night of her last auction in the Marketplace. When she had arrived with the usual erratic bats in her stomach, eyes glued to the heels of Marco's well-polished shoes, she didn't know it would be her last time on the block—although she desperately hoped it would be. Despite it being her third, she was terrified of auctions; the bright lights, the intense scrutiny, the silent freak outs; wondering which of the many hands that had probed, pinched, and tested her body would return in the end to claim her. And as always, by the conclusion of the night, she'd be so tense that her body would be on the verge of shaking and she on the brink of tears. In truth, if she weren't so distracted by trying to contain her nerves (and especially not embarrass her trainer) she would have noticed how tight and wonderfully sore her nipples always felt or how her pussy would swell and spread so prettily while her full thighs shone with her excitement.

Maybe if she had known that it would be her last time on the block, she might have appreciated it more. She might have treasured the feel of Marco prepping her, his nimble fingers priming her body while he issued reminders of proper conduct. She would have been especially thankful for the slight upturn of the corner of his mouth—the closest he'd ever come to giving an encouraging smile—before turning to walk out of her life again. She at least would have taken more pleasure in her careful surveys of the other slaves she was able to see (the only time she could really check out what other slaves looked like) enjoying and amazed at the variety. But she didn't know. So she knelt on that table, arms relaxed behind her, the ever-hated ball gag lodged between her lips, and prayed for the night to end.

It wasn't that she didn't appreciate the ritual of the auction. In fact, a good portion of her fantasies involved being kidnapped during some war or invasion by bandits, then sold to the highest bidder—which, of course would be some tyrannical king or rich warlord—and ultimately being forced to satisfy all his sexual needs. When she was younger, she spent many nights tying herself up in her bedroom, balled up socks in her mouth so her mother wouldn't hear her moans, jerking off while picturing herself being crudely displayed, as a crowd of hungry-eyed men called out numbers in order to claim her. But the reality of being on the block was a more daunting experience than she had anticipated, and not for the reasons one might think.

Davina was no fool. She fully understood she would have absolutely no control over who could purchase her. That, of course, was the whole point to being a slave. Ever since the day she discovered her stepfather's stash of magazines (oh, how those Japanese women were so beautifully tied!) she dreamt of an existence where she had no control. Being at the utmost mercy of another person appealed to her young mind in a way she could never explain and the need for it had only increased as she grew older. As she researched and eventually ventured out to play, she knew the only way to truly achieve it was to be a slave. But she also knew that to be one she should have no expectations... and for the most part, she didn't.

It really wasn't too selfish when she considered it. And it wasn't like she even had a type she preferred. She was happily bisexual, even though her experiences with women had been limited before training. She had long ago given up the romantic fantasies from her childhood and blissfully faced the unknown; not caring if her owners were rich, how they lived, what they preferred, how they played, how they punished... just as long as they used her, as long as they controlled her. But deep, deep in her heart, she had one flaw... just a single wish that made her mentally cross her fingers while she knelt on display: to avoid the wrong kind of owner.

Thankfully, the night did blur by. After a while, all the hands that touched her, all the appreciative and penetrating looks and steady thrumming of pain; it all blended together until her skin was slick and flushed, her thighs and ass hot with welts, and her heart thundering loudly in her chest. It had been the largest gathering of owners she had ever experienced, and she couldn't recall if her body had ever been so thoroughly and completely examined and explored. As she and the other slaves kept their positions, waiting for the bidding in the other room to be complete, she tried to will her ever-growing nerves to calm, knowing the next shoe was about to drop. Aside from a couple of uncertain people, she had felt more comfortable with this auction experience. Maybe it was the larger venue. Marco had promised the New York auction house would be lavish—and bigger meant a better selection of owners. She felt as nervous and agitated as she normally did, but as she considered the people who had spent the longest time poring over her file, despite herself, she started to relax.

It didn't take long for her to regret it.

As soon as the doors opened and the loud chatter began, she felt the bats return with a vengeance. She kept her eyes lowered, praying and hoping. But as soon as she heard it... the whistle that neared her table, she knew her lucky streak had officially ended. No longer able to maintain her control, her body started to tremble, even before she saw the hand reach for the collar around her neck, snapping shut the lock and removing the key. She could feel the tears at her eyes before the face came into view. She took in the dark hair with the touch of silver at the edges, the startling green eyes that looked like stolen gems, the smirk that clearly read, "You're mine."—and felt her throat go dry. She felt complete dread as the first significant moment of the night occurred.

And it was quickly followed by the second.

He leaned forward, the scent of him assaulting all her senses; woodsy, citrus, a touch of salt: masculine. His breath was hot on her cheek, his voice barely above a whisper yet weighted down with complete strength, "I've always wanted to own a pretty black girl."

It was the first time Davina was grateful for the ball gag in her mouth or she might have broken and cried out right then and there. She clamped her eyes shut, not believing the words she heard, hoping this was some mistake. There was no way this was happening to her. The absolute worst scenario she had envisioned since she discovered her desire for slavery had just unfolded and she felt sick. She started to take deep, strong breaths through her nose, willing everything to revert back and reset itself. This had to be some kind of nightmare. She was going to open her eyes and the whole picture would change. She was sure of it.

But when she did open her eyes, the emerald ones bore into hers with such ferocity, her ability to breathe suddenly failed her.

And that's when the third significant moment occurred.

Davina Warren considered leaving the Marketplace.

The drive to her new home took almost four hours. She sat on the floor of the limo while her new master sat comfortably in the leather seat, poring over papers from his briefcase, speaking to someone on a Bluetooth earpiece. He ignored her as he worked, and she was grateful, hoping to use the time to gather her wits and figure out what she was going to do.

For the first hour of the ride, Davina considered her options. Not once since she the day she discovered the Marketplace had she ever entertained the idea of leaving. After weeks of playing with Marco, she felt blessed to find someone who seemed to understand her needs. When he explained his position as a spotter/trainer and the secret world he represented, in her mind, she had already closed the door on her previous life. She felt no regret at cutting the frivolous ties, and for the first time she was grateful for the estranged relationship with her family. Giving up friendships, her job and her apartment was easier than she had thought. Truth be told, after she formally entered training she barely gave any of it a second thought. That she was now considering it was unfathomable.

Sneaking a look at her owner, she felt her stomach twist. Two whole years serving him seemed like an eternity and she wasn't sure how she'd be able to do it. But the alternative was walking away from her lifelong dream. To break her contract meant she'd have to leave the Marketplace for good. If she couldn't honor her duty, if she ran, then she'd pretty much be in exile. And the idea of going back to her old life was something she just couldn't imagine.

For the second hour, Davina berated herself. If she weren't so ungrateful, if she weren't so full of unnecessary pride, she wouldn't be in this predicament. Any slave would have appreciated the previous owners she had so carelessly left behind once the contracts had ended.

Her first, Master Delgado, had been an almost fabled version of the type of masters she had fantasized about. Dark features, handsome but not classically so, with an easy charm and the occasional cruel streak. In a large sprawling home, where there were three other slaves, it didn't take long for Davina to understand that her primary role was as his sexual release. Like the masters in her fantasies, he expected her to remain naked or scantily dressed and be available to spread her lips or legs at his command. Yet she couldn't consider herself a pleasure slave, because he didn't expect her to dazzle him with her wit and, in fact, rarely spoke to her unless it was instructions on which way to please him. And on occasion, when the mood struck, a strap or riding crop would appear in his hand and she'd endure short yet severe beatings, until he would finish by ejaculating all over her bruised skin. He rarely cared what she did with her time when she was out of his sight, and the elder slaves would keep her busy with cleaning and teaching her how to cook the array of Spanish delicacies their master enjoyed.

For the most part, she did enjoy her service with him, and when her contract ended after two years, she contemplated renewing. But the truth was—and this struck her as odd—she couldn't help feeling as if something was missing. Master Delgado was amazing and had seemed to fulfill everything she had looked for. She was most certainly being controlled. She was being delightfully used and her sole purpose was pleasing her owner. She felt no regret, so why did it still not feel right? So despite how much she loathed it, she took a chance and went to the block a second time.

The next person to purchase her was Brooke, who had taken Davina by blissful surprise. The woman who owned her couldn't have been more than five feet tall—definitely below Davina's five-foot-four frame—thin, almost bird-like, with a beautifully sculpted face and skin so pale, she was like walking milk. And her eyes... warm, golden brown and fringed with long, sweeping lashes, giving her a sweet, almost doll-like look. Where Master Delgado was a captivating charmer, by contrast Brooke was quiet and introverted. But in the privacy of her home she was one of the kinkiest souls Davina had ever encountered. There was only one other slave that Brooke owned, a tall, middle-aged Aussie named Riley who sent shivers down Davina's spine whenever he spoke, and on Davina's first night, Brooke had them fuck each other while she watched and masturbated.

"She's an interesting one," Riley had explained the following morning while they went over her duties. "Basically, the Missus is into having her own personal sex show. Got props, costumes, an' everything. She'll jump in, now and then, but she mainly likes to watch."

And true to his words, almost every day that first week Brooke had them perform for her, occasionally giving direction, putting Davina in positions she hadn't dreamed could be possible, while Brooke used various toys on herself as she watched. At first, Davina found herself feeling self-conscious, acutely aware of how her body moved and may appear. Yet, eventually, with Riley's aid, she began to enjoy it, allowing her mind to think of it as just another fantasy she was lucky enough to play out. And soon she began to throw herself into it, being playful and unabashed, giving her mistress the show that she deserved. And like Riley said, Brooke would sometimes have them join her in bed, allowing them to caress and stroke her body. Then she would either have Davina lick her to completion, or would climb on top of Riley and buck and grind on his dick until her body shook with her orgasm.

There was no question that Davina enjoyed being owned by Brooke. The sex was amazing, and as she and Riley were the only servants, she learned how to help manage the house and was finally able to use her skills from training. At last she had an owner who wanted her help in bathing, expected her to anticipate every need, and had her run just about every errand under the sun. But the best, the absolute highlight was that Brooke enjoyed seeing her slaves submit. Davina was happily on her knees again, took complete glee in kissing Brooke's feet and licking her dainty toes until her mistress quietly came above her. For the first time since she discovered the Marketplace, Davina was on cloud nine. She was a slave. And she finally felt like it.

But eventually—really, it made no sense—she again felt like something was lacking. She still enjoyed playing with (and especially for) Brooke, she adored being a real servant, and she truly did like Riley, who, despite the twenty-year difference in age, she had grown rather close with. However, the nagging feeling persisted and she began to wonder if she was just feeling antsy, like Marco suggested. Plenty of slaves jumped from contract to contract, liking the variety of serving different owners. It wasn't that Davina was opposed to it, but it just wasn't what she ultimately wanted. She had always envisioned herself finding that one person she'd serve until she didn't have another breath in her body to exhale. She wanted to contently devote her life to someone and couldn't see herself existing any other way. So even though she enjoyed her life with Brooke, and felt pangs at the thought of never kissing those pretty feet again, when her contract was up, she didn't renew.

And she went back to the block. Where her luck had apparently left her and she was now faced with serving a contract in the most unthinkable situation. And she had no one to blame but herself. This is what she deserved for not acting like a proper slave. For daring to have expectations. She had been owned, she had actually been the property of another person—two, in fact! Both were more than any slave could have hoped for. And she had felt they weren't enough.

The sound of fingers snapping broke through her fog of self-criticism. When Davina's eyes opened, she found her owner pointing to the space beside him on the expansive seat as he continued his conversation on the phone. She moved quickly, and as soon as she settled beside him, he pushed her back against the seat and with one hand undid the fly of her slacks.

He had moved so quickly, her breath caught in her throat as she felt his large hand slide under her black lace panties and cup her. It took every ounce of her strength to not cringe. Just the feel of his thick, blunt fingers pressing into her skin caused a more than uneasy feeling in the pit of her stomach. She ached to pull away, to scramble to the other side of the limo and put as much distance between them as possible.

The small cabin of the limo was filled with the steady thrumming of his voice as he continued with his conversation, and in fact, if his hand weren't trapped between her thighs, it would be as if she hadn't moved at all. With his free hand he continued shifting through papers, as the other slipped a finger between her thick lips, pressing against her clit. She couldn't stifle her gasp, and when he gave her flesh a firm squeeze, she bit her lip, chastened, and closed her eyes forcing her mind to fade somewhere else. All she had to do was get through it without embarrassing herself. Just concentrate on being what he deserved, what he purchased: a good slave.

That, she could do.

But oh, it was so hard! No matter how much she tried to sink into some fantasy that could help her get through this with some kind of dignity, she couldn't ignore what was happening between her legs. And no amount of imagination could mask who was touching her. As much as she tried, she couldn't help hear the small voice in the back of her head whisper, you're an embarrassment. She pushed the thought away, but when he slipped one wide finger inside of her, his entry almost effortless, her realization at how wet she already was caused her to go into a tailspin. How could she be enjoying this? Didn't she have any kind of pride at all? And in an almost defiant response, her hips lifted, grinding her clit into the heel of his hand, and her heart sank in abashment. You're nothing but a traitor, a complete disgrace. And she was. She couldn't deny it. What she had avoided most was happening and her body was responding like it didn't know any better. She truly was the sellout she had always feared.

When she was younger, it didn't take long for Davina to realize that her fantasies weren't exactly normal. Sitting in class during the day hearing horrific stories from history and spending nights pretending to be a ravaged, kidnapped victim was an irony that was not lost on her. Almost as soon as she gave in to practicing with stockings and neckties to imitate the women in the magazines, the guilt started. She felt as if she was glamorizing a very painful part of her people's history, and couldn't help feel something had to be wrong with her. None of her girlfriends mentioned wanting to do anything remotely similar with the boys they dated, and in fact, the very idea of a being with someone controlling was an absolute taboo.

It had taken her years to finally seek someone, the guilt ultimately being surpassed by her growing desires. Once she had settled in college, clear across the country in freeing California, she filled her spare time with chat groups, forums, and kinky personal ads, painstakingly looking for someone she could feel comfortable with. She wasn't exactly sure of what she wanted, but she was acutely aware of what she didn't. The only way she had been able to enjoy her depraved thoughts was by imagining her master as someone of color. An African warlord, an Arabian prince, maybe a cruel Japanese businessman. Her imagination gave her small comfort where the desire to be a slave already felt like betraying her own race. But to actually fantasize submitting to a white man—servicing him, being beaten by him, calling him... Master—to romanticize the very image of what she had been raised to loathe was too much. There were no words for the amount of shame she'd feel.

That was when her lucky streak had begun. She waded through numerous offers until she found a professional black couple who were both dominant, and after lengthy conversations she agreed to meet and then eventually play. After the first two hours she spent tied to their bed, a puddle of her come soaking the sheets beneath her, her pussy and ass completely numb, she knew there was no turning back; she had found her place in life. And when that relationship had played itself out, she felt comfortable enough to keep looking, finding other people equally as fun. Eventually the guilt wouldn't be as ripe, and as her playing got more serious as she looked for people who mirrored her desire for a more permanent situation, she eventually started feeling better. And by the time she met Marco at a weekend leather event, she had somehow managed to make peace with it.

That is, until her first auction.

❦

By the time Davina realized she was near orgasm, there were tears stinging her eyes. She had been so focused on keeping her emotions in check; she hadn't realized how her body was responding to his manipulations. Her hips had settled into a steady rocking motion, meeting his thrusts with eagerness she couldn't understand. She could feel her juices soaking through her panties and her clit was a hard pebble straining for his hand to press in harder as twinges of lightning shot through it. She was biting her lip to keep quiet, but each trip his finger made invoked a slight whimper from her throat. Go ahead, the voice taunted, you've already sold out, you might as well give it to him. The thought cut her like a knife and she could no longer hold back the tears. And just as she felt them start to creep down her cheeks, the twinges expanded and mushroomed; an explosion between her thighs that fractured, lighting her entire body afire. She pressed one fist against her lips as she erupted beside him, desperately trying to remain as quiet as possible to not interrupt his conversation.

But as her body started to calm, and he withdrew his hand, slick with her juices, whatever strength she had left to keep herself in check dissolved. And before she could stop it, a sob escaped her lips.

And that was when his voice paused.

Davina didn't need to look up to know that he was staring at her. She refused to look, trying in vain to stop her tears from flowing. She wiped her eyes with the edge of her sleeve, praying for the ability to get it together quickly enough before she angered him.

But it was too late. Still feeling his gaze on her, she heard him say, "Phillips, let me get back to you. There's something immediate I need to handle." After a few moments, she heard him end the call and for the first time since they entered the limo, there was silence. Complete and utter dread washed over her as she felt his gaze burn her. She knew she must look a mess, and even she could admit she wasn't the prettiest crier. At this very moment he was probably regretting purchasing her, and she couldn't blame him. If Marco saw her right now, he'd probably kick her for such an embarrassing display.

And when her new owner shifted in his seat, she knew he was probably in agreement with Marco. She saw his hand rise, and she braced herself, waiting for the first blow she knew in her heart she deserved. But instead, what she got was his hand grasping her wrist. Bewildered, Davina allowed herself to be pulled towards him and with his guidance she found herself lying across the seat, her head in his lap. She was confused as to what he wanted from her, until she felt his fingers stroking the side of her face.

And to her amazement, he gently said, "It's ok, let it out."

She blinked, unsure of what she had heard.

"Listen, little one," he continued. "Cry if you must. I'll allow this little outburst now, but after this, I expect you to act properly."

And despite her best efforts, the tears started to flow again, and this time she didn't try to hide them. Davina Warren cried. She curled up into a ball, pressed her face into the chest of her master and literally bawled.

And he let her. For the remainder of the car ride he cradled her while she cried out her shame, and when the tears finally ceased, he allowed her to stay, even when he returned to his work. By the time they arrived in Boston, she had managed to regain some of her composure and was, as she hoped, presentable when they reached his home.

He gave her a quick tour of the Beacon Hill brownstone, the last being the guest room that would be hers. And after issuing a few instructions on what her duties would be for the following morning, he gave a quick nod before walking out, closing the door behind him.

Davina sat on the plush bed, looking around the tastefully decorated room and made her decision. In her heart, she knew she was Marketplace. And a Marketplace slave had honor. After all it was only two years. No matter how uncomfortable it might be, she knew she could handle it. Only two years and then she could go back to the block or try for a private sale. If there was one thing she believed in, was that the right owner for her was out there. All she had to do was be patient.

With the decision finally reached, she relaxed and settled into bed and her new life.

Two Years Later

The first thing that crossed Davina's mind as she awoke was her impending call with Marco. Hitting the alarm to end its shrieking, she immediately pushed the thought out of her mind, knowing the heavy conversation about her contract would become too distracting if she dwelled on it. After a short but scalding shower, she started the coffee, making sure to gather everything that was necessary on the breakfast tray. It was Sunday, and on Sundays, he preferred to cook, so all she had to do was get the coffee and paper. Once everything was set, she carried the tray down the hall to his bedroom.

She found him sprawled on his back on his king-sized bed snoring loudly. After setting the tray on the bedside table, she gently unwound the blanket and sheets from his body, careful to not wake him. He was semi-hard, and after fitting a condom over him, she took him deep into her mouth, his head easily lodging in the entrance to her throat. She breathed deeply, relaxing it, readying it, and folded her arms behind her back. As she pressed her nose into the thicket of hair, inhaling his pungent scent, she settled into position and held still. She was not allowed to use her hands. She was not allowed to bob her head. She was not allowed to suck. Davina's master treasured the sensation of simply growing in her mouth as he woke, and the only thing she was to do was hold position, and keep her lips formed in a perfect O.

His dick stirred the moment it felt the warm enclosure made

by her lips. She felt it twitch, felt it jump, each movement triggering her nipples to answer by tightening. It was becoming hard to ignore the feel of them grow and fatten, gravity slightly tugging as her breasts hung below her. It wasn't difficult to hold the position, and more often than not he would keep her bent like this until the muscles in her stomach and jaw were so sore tears would fill her eyes. But her body was truly trying to sabotage her today, already aching to move. She so wanted to press her thighs together. Just a little bit. She wouldn't be greedy, only enough to give her some relief. But of course she never would. She wasn't the slave to cheat. Her curse was allowing her traitorous body to divert her attention from being perfect at her duties. So she had to ignore it, banish the growing sensations, so she could concentrate on the one thing that mattered: being a hole.

And, in fact, doing just that was actually the hardest part. Keeping completely still while he throbbed and pulsed in her mouth was an almost impossible task. As he thickened, spreading her lips, her tongue suffered, wanting to twist and coil and coax him along. And his balls were so close, growing firmer, their muskiness calling out for some attention. She wanted rub her cheeks against them, draw them between her lips and let them know how much she'd miss them. Oh, she was going to fail. Her eyes were tight as she forced herself to focus. She concentrated on her breaths; deep, calming breaths through the nose, keeping her throat as open and accommodating as possible. Like a good slave should. Like a good hole would be.

She knew he was awake when she felt the biting grip of his hand on her skull. He pressed her face somehow even deeper into his crotch as he stretched, a raspy half-yawn/half-groan invoking from him.

"Ahh, good morning, girl," He said, punctuating his statement with a quick thrust of his hips. His gruff, baritone voice, even traced with exhaustion, bounced off the walls resounding in her ear and she shivered.

He didn't expect an answer, so she remained still and continued to just breathe as he began to move. Always slow... always leisurely. Her master was a man of quality, of enjoying the sensuality of each moment. He rocked in and out of her mouth, unhurried, long and solid, his fingers roughly massaging her short curls. When he bottomed out, he would arch his back filling her completely; grinding himself into her face till her senses only registered him. There was no denying that she would miss this and she was surprised by how much. She had managed to hold herself in perfect position, and actually able to tune out the betraying sensation of her nipples, but couldn't deny the embarrassment at how wet her thighs were. And she knew he could smell it.

He did and responded by clamping two fingers around her nipples and squeezed. The gurgled sound that came from her throat only made him laugh and he continued, twisting, pulling, and pinching her hardened bud until her nerves were singing and begging, her breast heavy and tender. Oh how she wanted to move. Suck his dick, lick his balls, buck her hips; any would do, just as long as she could do something. And she was only becoming more wet. Her pussy felt absolutely swollen, and her juices were running down her thighs. She felt flush and knew if she weren't so dark, she'd be completely red from the humiliation.

"Always, always so easy, huh? Always ready to come." He chuckled, pressing her head down as he thrust upwards, his dick completely cutting off her airway. Even though it was unnecessary, she reminded herself to remain still. No matter how long it took, no matter how much she needed to breathe, she'd have to remain still. He was in so deep; she was able to feel his hardened balls against her cheek. Everything about her existence at that moment bulged in her throat, and briefly, she wondered if she could actually go.

"Well, you're not going to come." He said, shaking her head roughly. "I'm going to enjoy that pretty mouth of yours and fill it up. You're going to have to suffer and stay wet when you walk out that door. That will be your punishment for leaving me. Do you understand me?"

She gave a muffled noise in agreement, blinking away the

disappointment at not being able to gain relief. When he suddenly pulled her head up, until just the tip remained between her reddened and swollen lips, she almost whined in defiance. But he shoved her head back down and gave a long and loud sigh as he filled the condom. Her eyes fluttered closed as she relished in the feel of him shuddering beneath her, the grip on her hair so tight that it more than hurt, but she proudly kept her position and lovingly kept his dick encased while he softened.

When he released her, she gently pulled back, the pang of regret a slight sting. She quickly removed the condom and wiped him clean, taking care to straighten the bed sheets as she re-covered his lower half.

As she poured coffee into his mug, she noticed an envelope standing against the base of the lamp, and in neat handwriting read: For Davina, from Luke.

"Sir?" She asked, as she handed him the mug.

"Just a bonus. Extra cash. Take it and give me a kiss before you go," he said gruffly.

Davina tried to hide her smile as she leaned forward, planting a soft kiss on his cheek. As she pulled back, she took him in and felt a flutter of warmth in her stomach. He was truly a bear of a man. His broad, angular face had its usual grumpy façade, but she could see the twinkle of affection in his sparkling green eyes. And as always, a small habit that he had allowed from her, she gave his rounded, hairy belly a gentle rub before she backed out of the room, taking the envelope with her.

The rest of her morning flew by. She packed her suitcase, setting it by the front door before she quickly ran around the brownstone, straightening anything that seemed out of order. By the time Marco called, she had been sitting in her room, staring at the plane ticket in her hand for what seemed like the umpteenth time, and feeling rather pathetic about it.

When the phone rang, she grabbed it quickly and smiled when she heard Marco's silky greeting.

"So you sure you've thought this through? I don't want to

dissuade you, of course, but I just want to make sure."

"Yes." She replied, trying not to think of the taxi that would be at the door in about twenty minutes. "Trust me, Marco, I thought everything through. I'm ready."

"Ok, good. Well, it's pretty much the standard contract you already have now, except it'll be for five years. And hey—I know you said you wanted something longer, but trust me, just take it slow. This is your first renewal and I don't want you to overwhelm yourself."

She chuckled, knowing that despite what he said, she could handle it. "I know."

"Ok, so let's go over that new addition I mentioned earlier," he began.

She smiled as she listened, feeling just a slight relief at knowing that even though she was practically being forced to go on vacation, when she came back she'd be coming back to Him. And she'd continue to belong to Him. For as long as he wanted her. Mexico would be fun, but the true paradise was at her place, by his feet.

As his slave.

Foreword

While most of the writers in this collection were pleased to create new characters, I was pleased to see a few who brought back some established inhabitants of the world, even in cameo appearances. Their stories continue in my head, so why not in the heads of readers and writers? This next story endeavors to answer the eternal question, "And then what happened?" for a character I always thought was one of the nicest guys I had the pleasure to write about. I am thrilled that talented author D. L. King decided to whisk him away into another country, a first owner, a new house and life and outlook.

D. L. King spends an inordinate amount of time reading and writing smut in her New York City apartment and postage stamp-sized garden. She is the editor of *The Harder She Comes: Butch/Femme Erotica*, the IPPY gold medalist *Carnal Machines: Steampunk Erotica*, *The Sweetest Kiss: Ravishing Vampire Erotica*, *Spank!* and the Lambda Literary Award Finalist, *Where the Girls Are: Urban Lesbian Erotica*.

She publishes and edits the erotica review site, Erotica Revealed, which has been referred to as the *New York Times Book Review* of Erotica. The author of dozens of short stories, her work can be found in various editions of *Best Lesbian Erotica*, *Best Women's Erotica*, *The Mammoth Book of Best New Erotica* as well as anthologies such as *Yes, Ma'am, Please, Ma'am, Sweet Love, Fast Girls, Sex in the City: New York* and *Gotta Have It*, among many others. She is the author of two novels of female domination and male submission, *The Melinoe Project* and *The Art of Melinoe*.

Find out more about her at dlkingerotica.blogspot.com and dlkingerotica.com.

If You Try Sometime
D. L. King

"Here, put these on." The woman handed him the uniform he had worn previously when he had run errands with Chris. His heart was pounding a mile a minute. He barely heard her command. It was the regal quality and the English accent that stopped the white noise in his head and brought him back to the here and now.

Robert accepted the clothes and bowed his head. "Thank you, Madame."

"In future, if I should ask you a question or request your opinion, you may call me Madam. Is that clear?"

Without raising his head, Robert replied, "Yes, Madam." He couldn't believe he'd already fucked things up. How could he be so stupid? All the old fears began to cascade. In the middle of this reverie he felt a delicate hand wrap around his wilted cock.

"I understand. At a time like this, excitement, nerves, fear— can run high." She gently stroked him until he began to stiffen in her grasp. "That's better," she said. When he was hard again and his breathing had returned to normal, her grasp tightened painfully around him. She bent close to his ear. "As I say, I understand. This once. But it won't happen again." With a final tightening of her fingers, she quickly stood and let his cock spring up against his belly. "Once you are dressed, you may follow Emily out to the car and wait."

Emily drove. He'd had no idea where they were going and was a little surprised to find himself at the rental return at JFK Airport. He unloaded the bags from the trunk and loaded them into the shuttle to the terminal while Madam signed for the car. Once in the shuttle, she handed him his passport and told him they were booked in to the eight p.m. British Airways flight to London. "You and Emily will be on your own in Economy."

By the time they'd arrived at London's Heathrow Airport, Robert had learned a lot about Madam's household. He'd learned that she kept residences in both London and New York, but that she considered London to be her home. He'd learned that she kept three full-time slaves at the London townhouse and that he had been purchased to replace her former chauffeur. Emily was her secretary and there was an upstairs maid, whose name was Daisy. Madam also employed a cook who had full knowledge of the running of the house, but unlike so many lurid Victorian novels, Cook was really very sweet and never lifted a hand in punishment to a slave—neither, however, did she lift a hand to ameliorate any suffering.

Everyone had more than one duty. Daisy was both maid and ornament. Emily was both secretary and body slave. Georg, Madam's former chauffeur, had been her driver, handyman, and gardener.

Robert had begun to feel completely inadequate. Although he was very strong, he was no handyman and what he knew about gardening, you could put in a teacup; in fact, he knew a lot more about tea. He'd asked Emily why Georg had left but she said she didn't know. She said his contract had run out and he'd asked that it not be renewed. She didn't know whether he'd been resold or had left the Marketplace altogether. Unfortunately, Emily wasn't much for gossip.

Sleeping in coach was a virtual impossibility and he only managed to get in a few catnaps, so he arrived at Heathrow both exhausted from the trip and excited about his new life. Madam, who was a British subject, left Emily, who was Canadian, and Robert to their customs line.

"Stick with Emily; she knows where to go."

Almost an hour later, they joined Madam waiting by the taxi queue. Robert helped the cabbie load the luggage and helped Madam into the taxi. While Madam discussed house business with

Emily, Robert watched the sites go by out the window. They were soon left off in front of a beautiful and imposing three-story terraced house in Mayfair. The houses on the street all formed a sort of great wall, each virtually identical to the next with small exceptions, such as door color, brass makers, door hardware or knockers or interior draperies or a lack thereof.

Robert gathered the bags and followed the ladies inside. "My bags go to my suite on the second floor, Emily's bag to her rooms on the third floor and your bag to the last room to the left of the stairs on the third floor. Once you've take them up, I'll meet with you in the library."

Madam's suite was luxurious. The sitting room faced the front of the house, and the bedroom faced a lovely garden in the back. Robert knew he shouldn't have explored that much, but he couldn't help it. He left her three suitcases and a smaller carry-on at the foot of the bed. He looked at the space with longing, hoping that, one day, he might be allowed to sleep on the deep, wine carpet where he'd set down the bags.

He climbed the stairs with the rest of the luggage. Emily's rooms were very nice: small but comfortable. They included a small sitting room, bedroom, and bathroom. There were two large bookshelves, filled with books, a desk, and a television. He left her bag at the foot of the bed and continued down the hall to the last room on the left. It was a closet-sized room with a twin bed. There was an old, circular rug with a pattern of faded roses next to the bed and a wardrobe against the far wall. There was a bed table with a reading light and a small desk and hard backed chair. There was no attached bathroom. He left his bag on the bed and went downstairs.

Finding the library just to the right of the foyer, he entered and waited. Madam was speaking to a blond girl in a black and white, Victorian maid's uniform. Her hair was in a bun on top of her head and a white cotton accordioned cap sat in front of it. She wore a starched white blouse with a high, lace collar, a black skirt that reached her calves, and a pinafore with a square bodice and wide straps. She curtsied and left to stand by the door, passing Robert.

"Take those clothes off."

Robert's usual butterflies returned as he quickly stripped.

"Hand them to Daisy. She will dispose of them."

Dispose of them? Robert began to think of what might be in his suitcase, until he realized that he was Madam's slave; bought and paid for, contract signed. If she wanted him naked for the rest of his time with her, he'd be naked. That actually began to calm him some. Until he realized his nasty thing—no, his cock; he remembered his training—was becoming erect.

"Come over here; let me look at you." Madam, seated in a maroon wing chair rose as Robert came to stand in front of her. He stood, legs apart, hands behind his neck in a pose designed to display the body and make it easier for Madam to examine him. She slowly walked around him. "First things first," she said. "Stand in the center of the room, bend over and wrap your hands around your ankles."

Robert's cock began to vibrate in anticipation of what was to come and it wasn't disappointed when the first stripe from her cane turned from white to red. She laid stripe after stripe on his bottom and upper thighs, the caning made extra painful due to the tautness of his skin from his position. He received ten strokes, although it felt like so much more in the hand of such a masterful woman.

"You may straighten up," she said. "That was the punishment you were due for speaking out of turn yesterday in New York. I commend you on not having done it again, but rules must be upheld and protocol must not be broken. You take a caning quite well, though it may not be the best form of discipline for you, based on what I see here." Her thumb and index finger very lightly traced the length of his cock as it stood away from his body, pointing at a slight upward angle. "I do so love the cane, though," she said, giving the side of his cock a smack. "Well, we'll see."

She ran her hand through his chest hair, tweaking a nipple. "I like this." Her hand ran down his belly until her fingers were buried in his pubic hair. "But this will have to come off." She grabbed a handful of hair and pulled. She weighed his balls, then bounced them in her hand before gently slapping them. Making her way around him, her finger traced a few of the stripes she'd laid down on his backside. "Put your hands on the arm of the chair and move your legs back and apart."

Robert did as he was told, thrilled in the knowledge that he could once again shave, or maybe even wax the horrible, furry mat of hair between his legs. He'd gotten used to having chest hair again but he still hadn't got used to having that thick mass of pubic hair, and would be glad to see it go. His reverie ended when he felt her hands spread his cheeks apart.

"Yes, here too. Waxing will be best," she said, more to herself than to Robert. "You may stand up." Robert went back to the examination pose. "You may relax now. Arms at your sides. Have you ever been to England before?

"Yes, Madam, several years ago."

"Did you have opportunity to drive a car at that time?"

"No, Madam."

"Have you ever driven a right-hand drive vehicle?"

"No, Madam."

"Well, I certainly have no mind to place myself at risk of bodily harm. You will receive driving lessons from Emily, daily, for a period of one week, at which time I will expect you to take over all driving responsibilities. You will find chauffeur livery in the wardrobe in your room, as well as a comprehensive map book of London and its vicinity. You will wear the livery whenever you are driving or accompanying me out of the house. You may wear jeans when working in the garden but when you are in the house, you will be naked, unless I wish you otherwise.

"Now, I'm sure you're tired from your trip. You may go upstairs, have a bath and a lie down. Report to Cook at four o'clock for tea. You are dismissed."

Robert ran a hot bath in the upstairs bathroom, adding some

lavender scented bath oil both to help him relax and to moisturize his abraded rear end. The welts stung a bit when he first climbed into the tub, but the heat and scent finally soothed and calmed him and he luxuriated for much longer than he though was strictly proper. But Madam did say he had the rest of the morning and early afternoon to relax and the bath would help to calm him enough to actually fall asleep.

He awoke two hours later, in time to meet the cook in the kitchen. He was embarrassed to walk into the brightly lit workspace completely naked. After all, he was the only male in the house, and a very hairy one, at that. For her part, Cook was completely unfazed. She handed him a cheese sandwich and told him to sit at the table. His butt was still sore from the earlier caning and the hard wood of the chair served to focus his attention on that part of his anatomy.

Cook set a cup of tea with milk and sugar in front of him. "You're to meet Madam in the cellar at a quarter past."

The cellar sounded ominous and Robert's cock twitched. After finishing his sandwich, Cook pointed him in the direction of the cellar stairs and he made his way down. The stone floor was cold on his bare feet, but felt dry. The floor below ground was nothing like he'd imagined, however, as it was well-lit and heated, even if the heat didn't quite reach the floor. Once past the stairs, he found himself in a large, open space. He noticed a washer and dryer, along with a folding table and hanging rack off to the side and three closed doors spaced out around the perimeter.

One of the doors opened and Madam stepped out of the room. "Ah, here you are. Come along." She ushered him into the room she'd just exited. "Ruth had some time this afternoon so she's come to take care of your grooming needs. Up here now." She patted an oxblood leather table with cuffs attached at the top and bottom along with various tie down points along the sides. "I assume you've been waxed before?"

"Yes, Madam," Robert said, looking around the room. It appeared to be a playroom, with various pieces of heavy, dark wood furnishings. He noticed a rack holding canes of various sizes against the far wall and rows of paddles, taweses, straps, floggers, and whips hanging on the wall above.

"Can you hold still or do you need to be restrained?"

"Madam?"

"Yes, it's all very interesting, but Ruth only has two hours to spend with you. Can you hold still while you're groomed?"

"Yes, Madam," Robert said.

"Good. I'd be very disappointed to find you weren't trained well enough to control yourself under these simple circumstances. We'll start with the back first. On your stomach, now."

Robert turned over and spread his legs. He heard footsteps and a wheeled cart and then felt a warm hand on his bottom, fingers spread his cheeks apart. Soon he felt the hot wax spread just inside his exposed crack and the linen strip laid down then ripped off. It felt wonderful and brought back happy memories of being clean. He sighed against the leather table.

Ruth made quick work of his backside from just above the curve of his ass to a few inched below the start of his thighs and everything hiding inside the crack before she cleaned off the stray wax and had him turn over. His eyes felt slightly unfocused as he continued to sink deeper into his submission. Ruth was young and blond and attractive. She ran a comb through his pubic hair and then trimmed it to a more manageable length before slathering on the wax just above his penis. She laid down the linen strip and smoothed it against him and then, without any warning, she ripped it off. It came away black with matted hair and, if his nerves were telling the truth, a layer of skin, or so it felt.

It had been a while since he'd been waxed with a full growth of hair and he'd forgotten how painful it could be. But again, the pain was comforting. By the time Ruth had completely removed all the hair, his eyes were tearing freely, but he had a huge smile on his face. "Thank you," he said, then quickly looked over to where Madam had been standing, sure he'd made another mistake.

"No, that's perfectly acceptable. You should thank Ruth for her handiwork." Ruth smiled down at him as she cleaned up the bits of wax sticking to his skin and rubbed lotion in. "Of course, she's not finished yet," Madam said as she ran her fingers over his newly waxed skin, pressing against it here and there. "I said she would be here for two hours and it's scarcely been twenty minutes." She stroked the area between his legs and up against the root of his cock as it strained upward, pre come dribbling from the tip. "Now she has to do the balls. And those won't be waxed." Madam gently circled his cock before squeezing it just as he felt the searing pain of a single hair being pulled from the skin on his testicles. He couldn't help it; there was an involuntary jump in the muscles of his right leg.

"Oh, and you were doing so well," Madam said. She quickly cuffed his ankles to the sides of the table and for the next hour and a half, Ruth tortured him with her tweezers. She pulled out one hair after another until his balls were completely devoid of even peach fuzz and red as any of the welts on the back of his ass. About fifteen minutes in, Madam stuffed a ball gag in his mouth. He couldn't remember screaming, yelling or otherwise making noise, but he must have been. But of course, as was always the case, the bondage helped him to relax into the pain and let himself go, so that by the time Ruth was finished, he was flying high, but still present enough to marvel at the way his poor sac felt as Madam bathed it in the fluid warmth of her mouth.

Even after she stopped and removed the gag, he could still feel her tender tongue caressing his freshly depilated balls. Tears of gratitude blurred his vision as he thanked her.

Months later he'd become used to the sessions with Ruth. The waxing ceased to hurt, but the tweezers always did. By the third session he no longer had to be restrained or gagged and took the treatment like a man (as he became fond of thinking). But Madam never anointed his balls again. He understood, of course, but it didn't stop him longing for her mouth. And it wasn't as though she never touched him; that was far from the case. She was just seldom quite that intimate again.

Robert loved driving the Bentley and easily settled into driving Madam to various appointments, the sales, teas, lunches with friends, anywhere, really. He was absolutely suited to Madam's world. It was a far cry from running his own company but he finally felt like he fit in the world and he was even rewarded, from time to time, with Madam's caning expertise.

❦

Madam hadn't had cause to punish him in months, but she had come up with the perfect punishment, for those times it was necessary. She'd discovered, purely by accident, that humiliation was Robert's Achilles' heel, and not just any kind of humiliation, but a very particular form of humiliation.

She'd known his old mistress, had even seen him at her house. She'd never liked the woman, or approved of her favorite sport. She'd remembered Robert as someone who might have been attractive if he hadn't been tarted up as the ugliest sissy on the face of the planet. Madam thought that under the sissy trappings, he might actually be quite virile. She had much better uses for a body like that.

She'd been happy to find him again at Alex's, and happier still to find that Alex had managed to purge him of the personality his old mistress had induced in him. As soon as she'd seen his file, she'd known she would buy him. And she'd been very happy with him. He was extremely intelligent, strong, a good driver, equal to her roughest games, and his cock was something special. His gardening left something to be desired and he wasn't particularly handy but he was learning. She'd discovered, almost by accident, the thing that upset him the most—and it was all thanks to Alex's training.

One day, early on, while driving her home, he'd failed to look in the correct direction before turning and they'd come very close to being hit by an oncoming car. He'd squealed like a girl and hugged himself. Of course, he'd got hold of himself right away and managed to drive her home in one piece, but she felt the need to punish him, more for his behavior than the almost accident.

Making the punishment fit the crime, she'd given him a leopard skin bra and matching panties. She'd put a truly ugly wig on his head and smeared red lipstick on his mouth. "If you're going to act like a silly girl, you might as well look like one. Go sit in the corner and cry." And he had cried. She could tell that he was absolutely miserable. She ignored him for two hours, and during that time, a change had come over him.

Later, she'd asked him about it and he'd told her he'd had an epiphany. He'd come to understand, once and for all, that the life he'd worked so hard to have, before the Marketplace, was not at all the life he wanted. Certainly, he wanted to be dominated by a strong woman just as much now as he had then, but he didn't want to be an emasculated sissy; he wanted to be a man.

She had to hand it to Alex and Grendel; through their hard work, he'd not only been made a useful addition to the Marketplace but, just like the Stones song, Robert had got what he needed, which had, in turn, given her exactly what she needed, as well.

Foreword

From the serene order of a personalized, structured household I turn you to another perspective. The Marketplace lends itself to tales of slaves finding themselves in strange, foreign, and frightening settings; after all, they are the commodities of the system, unable to choose where they go and into whose hands they will be trusted. But what happens when a new owner walks into a house full of slaves she did not choose, perfectly aware of her duties and responsibilities but a stranger to a staff accustomed to a radically different sort of ownership? Knowing what to do isn't enough; to control, to own, to dominate, one has to find... her own voice. Especially when she has a very particular taste in service.

After a long unproductive spell, Leigh Ann Hildebrand is overjoyed to be returning to print and reclaiming her self-identity as a writer. Her first short story sale was also to Laura Antoniou; she appeared in the anthology *No Other Tribute*. She also wrote for *The Sandmutopia Guardian* and *Growing Pains*.

Leigh Ann is bi-coastal and identifies as Neoclassical leather— which is just a fancy way to say 'Middle-Aged Guard.' She has been a Marketplace fan for so long that her original copy of *The Trainer* was an unbound pre-release manuscript. When she's not daydreaming about polishing Alexandra Selador's bathroom fixtures, Leigh Ann is a grad student training to be a pagan theologian.

Her Owner's Voice
Leigh Ann Hildebrand

Elaine O'Keeffe stood in the foyer of her father's house and looked at herself in the huge gilded mirror hanging there. The matte fabric of her modest little black dress made her skin look especially pale while the black hat sweeping her forehead drew attention to the redness in her eyes. I suppose I am a sight for sore eyes, she thought as she reached up to remove the hat. Just as she started to slide the hatpin out, a tall blonde woman in a plain black maid's uniform glided into view beside her in the mirror.

"May I take that for you, Miss?" the woman said, her face a mask of solemnity, her voice polite but loud in the silence of the bare foyer.

Elaine startled at the sound, but nodded slightly and allowed the hat to be removed and her auburn pageboy bob to be smoothed back into place by the woman. Within the mirror, Elaine watched herself being tidied and adjusted like a porcelain doll. She sighed and looked away before the other woman noticed she was watching.

"Cook is preparing a light supper to be laid out in the small dining room," the woman said, turning slightly towards one of the doorways off the foyer. "In anticipation of your return, of course. But perhaps Miss would rather rest first and have supper after?"

"After..." Elaine echoed softly. After the unexpected phone summons to the hospital, after tense conversations with cardiologists and surgeons, after heroic measures, after the funeral director and the viewing and the endless cups of tea and finger sandwiches, after the service with four eulogies and banks of gladiolas and carnations in extravagant arrangements, after the solemn graveside burial punctuated with the occasional sob from one of the servants, after the luncheon and the murmured condolences and the increasingly rowdy toasts, after hours turned to endless numbing days of ritual and hospitality—after it all, Elaine had to admit that she was exhausted.

"I... yes, I think I want to rest. The whole day has been so tiring," Elaine's voice trailed off. But Daddy's laid to rest, she thought to herself. Next to Mother, next to every other O'Keeffe up the whole family tree, God bless them.

The other woman shifted on her feet very slightly, betraying a hint of impatience. "I have already had the day bed in your rooms turned down, Miss. Is there anything else that I—that we can do for you?"

"No, that'll be fine," Elaine responded, and started through the foyer to the grand staircase. Before she had even started up the stairs, the other woman had turned to go, her impatience giving way to motion. "Wait, yes, there is something..." she began softly.

"Miss?"

"I think... I would like it if perhaps Daddy's secretary could see about flights to New York next week."

"Of course, Miss. I will have her sent up in 90 minutes?"

Elaine nodded. "I suppose 90 minutes is enough for a nap," she agreed half-heartedly. "And... have her wear clothes, please. Street clothes."

"Mourning, I imagine you mean, Miss."

"Sure, yes. Mourning. Black. In 90 minutes. Please see to it," Elaine said wearily and then continued up the stairs to her corner of the vast house. All through the halls, the drapes were pulled. The resulting gloom enveloped the house in a shadowy somberness like something out of a Gothic novel. Even her usually sunny private parlor was awash in gray. On the other hand, the daybed's white linens provided at least a spot of color in the dimness. Elaine mechanically removed her black pumps and slipped between the covers without bothering to change out of her dress. Within minutes, she was asleep.

It was twilight when she was awakened by a tapping on the door and a voice calling—a bit too loudly—"Miss? Miss? Miss Elaine?" Yawning widely, Elaine sat up and smoothed her hair, tucking it behind her ears.

"Mmm, come in," she said softly. There was no response. "Come in!" she repeated more insistently. In answer, a tall honey blonde in a black sheath dress and stiletto heels pushed the door open and walked briskly into the room. She had the tawny swimsuit model looks that Elaine's father had preferred when rewarding himself with a new slave. For a while, that had happened so often that they'd blurred together in Elaine's memory; she searched for this one's name. The woman had been purchased recently enough that Elaine had only seen her once or twice in passing during brief visits to the house for holiday dinners. On those rare occasions, the woman had been naked except for a collar—and heels, of course. Christine? Chrissie? No... Kristin, Elaine thought. That was it. She nodded at the blonde as she rose from the day bed and crossed to her little writing desk.

"Let me see," she began softly as she took a seat. "I'd like you to make arrangements for me to visit a friend of my father's next week. They're on Long Island. Perhaps flights to JFK, a hotel—there's a place in Woodbury I've stayed, or maybe a beach rental? Probably for a week. Oh, and limo service from the airport and..." Elaine's voice trailed off as she looked expectantly at the other woman, who had an uncertain expression on her face.

"I guess I should have given you time to start writing this down," Elaine said gently, noticing for the first time the how puffy and red the other woman's eyes looked.

"Ohhh, Miss, I'm... I'm sorry," Kristin began, looking genuinely uncomfortable. "It's just that I... I'm not... I mean, Sir—Mr. O'Keeffe—your father—he... well, I'm not that kind of secretary!" she blurted finally, coloring slightly.

"What kind of secretary are you then?" Elaine said already anticipating the answer.

Kristin wiggled almost imperceptibly in response, a kind of shiver running down her body and accentuating her breasts and hips with just the smallest of movements. "The bent-over-the-desk kind?" Kristin suggested, apologetically.

Elaine pursed her lips.

"You know, Sir—Mr. O'Keeffe—he was mostly retired from practicing law the past few years. He went in to the office just to be friendly and see everyone, and he liked... he wanted his old business friends to see me as a 'pretty young thing,' he told me." Kristin shook out her hair and turned her head a little towards one shoulder. "And then at home..."

"At home you were basically a pleasure slave."

Kristin nodded.

"Well, that's... less than useful," Elaine murmured. She took a piece of stationery from the desk drawer and wrote something on it, then held the page out to the other woman. "That's my travel agent. If you could call him and make the arrangements, it would be fine for now."

Kristin sniffed slightly as she took the paper. "Maybe if you wrote that other parts down? I wouldn't want to make a mistake and it's really not my place, Miss..."

Elaine blinked and took a slow breath. "Just call the number and have him call me. Do you think that would be possible?" She started to say something else, to ask what Kristin thought her place was now that her previous owner was dead—but the sadness in the slave's eyes kept Elaine from adding more.

Kristin nodded. "Yes, of course, Miss. I would be glad to do that for you." With that, she turned abruptly and left the room.

Elaine watched her model-stomp down the hallway until she disappeared from view, and then took more paper from the writing desk. "Dear Ms. Selador," she began. "Thank you so much for your heartfelt words of condolence on the death of my beloved father, Thomas Beauchamp O'Keeffe. He often spoke of you and Mr. Elliot fondly and treasured every slave you ever trained on his behalf..."

☙

A week later, Elaine found herself sitting at a small circular table in a cheerful solarium overlooking a green expanse of lawn. Next to her sat the lady of the house, Alexandra Selador herself, her soft wavy hair shining pale blonde and white in the sunlight. Spread out on the table in front of the two women were almost a dozen files containing headshots, notes, and other documents pertaining to each slave's history, health, and level of experience.

"Thank you again for seeing me on such short notice, Alexandra," Elaine said as she flipped through one of the files. "I know how difficult it must have been to pull together this many candidates so quickly, especially given the particulars."

Alex smiled gently at the young woman. "Thom O'Keeffe was a great friend to us from our earliest days as a training house. And your mother was a lovely woman, too."

Elaine nodded. "Mother used to say you could measure Daddy's successes in slaves; I think he must have come to you any time he wanted to celebrate some big litigation win. But at this point, all of it... the estate, the slaves..."

"It must be overwhelming to take on so suddenly."

"That... and... well, I mean, it's not that I never saw myself owning—it's part of the family now, I guess—but that I never imagined it like that."

Alex chuckled softly. "I guess it's not for everyone, estate living. Your mother use to say that Thom was compensating for a tar-paper shack childhood."

Elaine smiled and nodded thoughtfully. "I don't know what he was compensating for, but I don't think it was that bad. He did like making a show, didn't he? My theory is that he wanted to be Gerald O'Hara in Gone with the Wind."

Alex laughed: a pleasant musical sound.

"No, really! He wanted to be that blustery genial plantation owner and... well, let's just say he used to call me 'Katie Elaine O'Keeffe' when he was in a teasing mood and going on about land being the only thing that mattered. I am pretty sure if he'd had his way, I'd have been named Scarlett—but Mother had more sense than that."

Elaine fell silent for a moment, her eyes suddenly brimming

with tears.

"Sometimes, I really wish I could have been that daughter he wanted, the flirty, vivacious owner—in a corset, wielding a dressage whip and striding through the beautiful fantasy household he'd built, leaving a trail of broken hearts and bruised asses behind me. But instead of Scarlett, he got Melanie Hamilton."

Alexandra reached out and took Elaine's hand gently in her own. They sat in the silence for a few moments.

When Elaine had regained her composure, Alex brushed her hand across the files laid out in front of them. "So, what do you think of these?"

Elaine flipped through one of the files, pausing to glance at photos, medical notes, and handwriting samples. She pulled a small SD memory card from a pocket in the folder and held it up to Alexandra.

"Can I hear this one?"

Alex nodded and held it up beside her. A woman in a plain gray shift and a collar appeared at her side and took the SD card from Alex's fingers with a nod. In a moment the room echoed with a silvery masculine voice. "Lorem ipsum dolor sit amet, consectetur adipisicing elit..."

Elaine cocked her head and listened as the nonsense words continued. "He's hiding some kind of accent..."

Alex flipped through the pages of the file. "North Carolinian. He's had acting lessons; that's probably what you're hearing."

"His handwriting looks cramped."

"I'm sure it could be fixed with training."

Elaine sighed and picked up another file and began examining a life-sized photo of the client's right hand. She matched her fingers against the image thoughtfully. "This one has 22 years of service, most of it in Spain..." She set down the file again. "No, I don't know... not quite it."

She flipped a few pages and then continued. "Daddy's house— you don't know—it's like—well, the whole staff just runs on rails. I feel mowed down sometimes. They call me Miss."

Alex cocked an eyebrow. "Hmm?"

"Miss. They call me Miss, or sometimes 'Miss Elaine'—like I was a debutante. I'm 32 years old, and they're still calling me Miss."

The older woman looked more serious. "Elaine, you have to take them in hand. Make it clear to them that you're the owner now—or else you have to let them go to freedom or the block. It's not good for any of you otherwise."

"I think maybe they just have bad habits. Daddy was accustomed to letting them just do, letting the senior slaves run things. As long as he got what he wanted, I don't think he really cared how it was getting done."

"Your father had a reputation as a good owner, dear—and not just from slaves. We've had a long relationship with him, trainers liked him—"

Elaine nodded. "I'm not saying he wasn't a good owner. It's just that I'm not like that. I am not like him, or like he was with them. Daddy filled the whole house with his laughter and endless stories about cases and Marketplace goings on. His slaves are like that, too— I feel like they're always filling up space with talking, with noise. I don't... well..." She trailed off and gestured to the files. "I want something that isn't like that, something of my own. Something that's more like me. And now I... I can afford it," she finished, sighing.

Alex leaned back and assessed the younger woman thoughtfully. "Why don't you give me a week to bring in the three best candidates I can find? Then you'll come in and meet them, and decide then. Will you trust me with that?"

Elaine nodded with relief. "Of course I trust you, Alexandra!"

"Excellent. So, I'll give you a call when we're ready to meet."

The following week the two women met in a more formal parlor and shared tea and scones while they interviewed Alexandra's handpicked candidates. The first was already in front of them. At Elaine's request, he was seated in a plain straight-backed chair rather than kneeling. He was young and blond with a tall lanky body that made the chair look oddly small.

Elaine eyed him appraisingly and commented to Alex in a chatty tone, "He'd fit right in with the other tall blondes in the household, but only four years in service?"

Alex tilted her head. "Three, but they were in a diplomat's household, so he's had extra training. Oh, and Mark has very nice recommendations, don't you, dear?"

The young man blushed and nodded. He started opened his mouth to say something then closed his lips tightly.

"Good boy, remembering the rules," Alex said briskly. "Elaine, any other questions?" "Hands," she replied in a soft but firm tone.

He responded by holding out his hands flat and parallel to the floor, palms down. The nails were glossy and cut down to the quick, the cuticles smooth.

"Over."

He complied by turning over his hands so that the palms faced up. His fingers trembled slightly.

"Now," Elaine said, her eyes on his face, "tell me a bedtime story."

Mark glanced at the ceiling nervously and then closed his eyes briefly. Looking up again, he began in a surprisingly rich baritone. "Once upon a time in an ancient stone tower on the edge of a forest, a beautiful princess lived alone with her elderly mother and father. One day, through the high windows of the tower, she heard a strange melody wafting through the trees—"

"Thank you, that's enough." Elaine said as she leaned back in her chair. "That's all."

Alex made a note in the file. "Thank you, Mark. You can send in the next client. I'll be in touch," she said without glancing up.

He untangled himself from the chair and bowed slightly to the women before departing. When the door shut behind him, Alex looked quizzically at Elaine, who shook her head.

"No. And I don't know why."

The door opened again, and a distinguished older man entered and closed the door softly behind him before joining the two women. His neatly trimmed goatee was almost entirely gray; he wore a charcoal grey suit with a solid burgundy tie and matching pocket square.

"Elaine, this is Randall. Randall, are you clear on the terms of service Ms. O'Keeffe desires?"

His eyes seemed to twinkle mischievously as he nodded with a slight smile.

On the small note pad in her lap, Elaine wrote the word 'avuncular' and underlined it forcefully. She slipped a note card from between the pages and handed it to Randall.

"Read, please."

He held the card in his left hand and slipped his right hand into his breast pocket to pull out a pair of reading glasses.

Elaine shot Alexandra a concerned look.

"Lorem ipsum dolor sit amet," he read slowly in a measured British accent that made him sound like he'd shared the stage with Gielgud and Olivier. "...consectetur adipiscing elit. Nam ullamcorper ipsum nec enim rhoncus eget condimentum nisl ullamcorper." The words sounded surprisingly poignant.

Alex looked at Elaine. Her eyes were closed and she was smiling slightly. When she opened them again, she did so with a slight shake of her head. Nice, Elaine mouthed to the other woman.

Alex smiled in return. "Anything else you'd like to ask, Elaine?"

"No, that will be all. Thank you," she said in a soft clear tone.

Alexandra moved her hand in a small dismissive gesture and the man bowed gracefully and gave a firm nod and a smile to both women. "Please tell the last client we're ready for him," Alex said as he walked smoothly towards the door.

As soon as the door shut, Elaine burst out giggling. "It would be like having Kris Kringle as my personal slave!"

"He's very charming and very skilled, I can assure you," Alex said, grinning. "I say this from experience. You could do far worse. He'd need very little training to handle everything you'd asked for. I think he's probably the most suited of the three."

Elaine nodded in agreement. "I could hear that. His voice is exactly what I'm looking for. 'Nice' doesn't really cover it, does it? It's the kind of voice I'd want to own, to control, and maybe even to show off—like another woman might cage and show off her favorite slave's cock. But what would people say, Alex? I just lost my father! It'll look like I have some serious daddy issues."

"Don't you?"

The younger woman cleared her throat. "Not like that I don't. Besides, he'll be wanting to retire from service entirely before too long."

"Now, that's a valid concern," Alex agreed. The door opened for the final candidate. He paused in the doorway until Alex motioned with one finger to the chair. He took a seat on the edge of the chair, as if uncomfortable with the position. His eyes were downcast, but his back was straight; he sat with both feet squarely on the floor in front of him. For a few moments there was no noise in the room except for breathing.

Elaine leaned back to look at him. He was her age or maybe older—she couldn't tell without looking at his file—with wavy dark hair pulled back in a low ponytail and steel-rimmed glasses. She glanced over at the file lying open in Alex's lap before looking up at Alex.

"Evan. This would be his second Marketplace contract. Before that—well, he wouldn't be here if I didn't think he was a strong choice," Alex said, the last words emphasized.

As if in response, the man stretched out his hands along the top of his thighs. They were wider than those of the two previous men, with thick fingers. Like Mark's, Evan's nails were manicured to the quick. His hands flexed slightly, betraying a hint of nervousness. His gazed remained on the floor.

Elaine inhaled sharply. "Tell me a bedtime story."

The man looked up immediately, revealing olive green eyes fringed by thick dark lashes. He gazed intently at Elaine and took a long breath. His tongue flicked his upper lip briefly; then he began to speak softly.

"Once of a time, the king and queen of the Connacht were lying in their royal bed late at night when the king said to the queen, 'Are you not blessed to be the wife of a rich man?' The mighty queen laughed at her husband and said, 'Yes, but I was rich before I met you. I am a queen in my own right, my husband. My father was high king and I am the noblest and richest of all his noble daughters. I sought a man on whom I could bestow my family's honors and riches, and in time chose you. Is it not true that you are blessed to be the husband of a rich woman?'"

He paused to take a slow breath. Elaine raised the fingers of one hand slightly from their resting place on her lap. After a long second Evan blinked and leaned back slightly.

Elaine cleared her throat and looked down at her notes. "Thank you."

Alex shuffled a page in the file on her lap and closed the cover. "That will be all. I'll be in touch, Evan." He rose and tilted his head at both women, raising his eyes again to look at Elaine before turning. He shut the parlor door behind him inaudibly.

"I want him. How soon?" Elaine said firmly as soon as Evan had gone.

Startled with Elaine's sudden enthusiasm, Alexandra Selador chuckled as she opened the file again and began jotting notes. "Two weeks of intensive work in a couple of deficient areas. It'll be expensive."

Elaine shook her head. "I don't care how much. The tailor will need his measurements. And of course the paperwork, the contract, your fee..." Her hands fluttered nervously in her lap. "Honestly, I've never done this myself before; I only vaguely know what we do next from attending auctions with Daddy."

Alex put down her pen and offered her hand to the younger woman. "It's going to be fine." She paused thoughtfully. "May I ask...?"

Elaine turned a deep shade of pink and shook her head. "I don't know! It was just like when I didn't like that first one—Mark? It was... a gut feeling?"

Alexandra nodded. "Mmhmm. After years of doing this, I sometimes feel that spark when meeting a potential client. I know. One of the great mysteries of training, I suppose." She took a few more notes and then closed the file. "And you're sure that this is what you want? This contract, these limits?"

"I've thought about it a lot, Alexandra," Elaine replied. "I may not like the way Daddy handled slaves, but he taught me that ownership lives in particulars; owning means having exactly who and what you want, exactly how you want it. I guess he wanted to fill the estate with willowy blondes—loud blondes. I think he'd be pleased to see me being particular about my desires, too."

Alex smiled and rubbed her hand along Elaine's arm in a gently maternal gesture. "Fine, but if I'm going to meet our ambitious timetable, I need to get busy with Evan. I apologize for cutting the rest of our afternoon short, Elaine."

The younger woman rose and embraced Alex. "It's always a pleasure, even if it's a bittersweet one just now."

"It is a pleasure—and an honor for our house to continue working with the O'Keeffes! I'll be in touch with the details as soon as possible. In the meantime, I'm going to send you some reading material: things Parker has written that you might find helpful."

Two weeks to the day after the interviews, Elaine was back in her father's house—no, her house—having tea in the breakfast room and reading a white paper titled Effective Ownership in an Estate Setting that Alexandra had sent to her. Kristin—still in stilettos—clattered onto the room's Italian tile and announced abruptly that the new slave had arrived from the airport and was waiting in the foyer. Elaine finished up her toast and gathered up her reading while the slave shifted from one foot to another impatiently. After waiting an extra moment just to see the look of expectation on Kristin's face, Elaine rose and followed the faint sound of voices down the hallway to the foyer. When she arrived, almost a dozen other slaves were already there, chattering about the arrival so noisily that Elaine could barely resist covering her ears.

"Please!" Elaine said exasperatedly, "Surely some of you have duties or... something. See to them." The slaves responded by leaving the foyer proper, but peeked around the wide arched doorways that opened onto it.

Evan stood next to the door, an inscrutable expression on his face. As soon as he saw Elaine, he nodded in acknowledgment and then dropped his gaze to the floor. At his feet was a small duffel bag with all the belongings he'd brought with him.

"This is Evan," Elaine announced to the room for the benefit of the slaves she knew were listening. "He will be my amanuensis—my personal secretary. According to the terms of his contract with me, he is forbidden to speak or make any noise without my explicit permission." She paused to let that sink in. Evan's eyes flicked up at hers for a moment, and then back to the floor. "I know that's going to be a challenge to the way you all do things, but I am sure we'll make it work." Her voice echoed in the foyer. "Please see that he has a bed in the slaves' quarters and... get him settled in..." she trailed off, suddenly uncertain of herself again.

The foyer was silent for a moment before erupting in motion and noise that echoed harshly on the marble floor.

"Of course, Miss," she heard. Kristin giggled from one of the doorways. Her father's housekeeper, a brisk, angular woman, stepped out of the front parlor's doorway and motioned to Evan as she spoke. "We'll get him taken care of. And then you'll want him sent up, I imagine? In an hour, I would expect?"

Elaine nodded assent in a passive, mechanical way and then remembered herself. "Yes, Mrs. ...Burke," she responded with unpracticed authority. "Please have Evan in my room in an hour."

From near the staircase, Elaine thought she heard a snicker. She glanced in that direction where several male slaves she didn't recognize were leaning against the mahogany stair rail. Good grief, she thought. I have footmen. Shouldn't there be a butler supervising them? Who are these people? She had read through the thick stack of contracts once, noting end dates, but as yet hadn't attacked the actual organization of the staff. No doubt she would need to meet with them all, and soon. She sighed and flexed her jaw. "I will be busy with correspondence," she said softly, trying not to sound too defensive as she fled up the stairs to the quiet safety of her own parlor.

An hour later, there was a soft tapping at her door.

"Come in," she said softly. Evan pushed the door open slowly. He had changed into his new 'uniform'—a soft hunter green silk shirt and dark pants. Elaine set aside the white paper she'd still been finishing up when he arrived. "Let me see you," she said, spinning her finger around in the air.

Evan walked towards the center of the room; he turned in a slow circle, his black leather-soled slippers silent on the carpet. When he was facing her again, he raised an eyebrow and caught her eye before looking down again.

"Yes, I like it. The sleeves may have to be less full, though. Sit, please," she said, motioning to the floor beside her chair. Evan knelt next to her and tilted his head slightly in a gesture of attentiveness.

"I know you've read the contract and have the countersigned copy. For the next two years, your voice belongs to me," she said gently. "You have agreed that you will not say anything to anyone but me, and to me only with my consent. You may not make any voluntary noises; this includes moans or cries of pain, no matter what the circumstances. You will continue learning ASL to use in appropriate situations; eventually I will hire or buy an instructor for the entire staff," she said, remembering the chatter at Evan's arrival. "In the meantime, you may use a notepad to communicate with the rest of the household when necessary."

At that, Evan slipped a hand into his pocket and retrieved a set of note cards in a flat leather case, which he offered up to Elaine mutely.

"Yes, that will do," she said. "And…let me see your script."

Evan reached into his other pocket and pulled out a pen, then began to write on the top card in the little leather holder. When he was done, he held it out for her. She took it from him gently. In a beautiful vintage style he had written, "The quick brown fox jumped over the lazy slave." When she looked up at him, he had one eyebrow cocked at her questioningly.

"Yes, I like it," she responded, tracing her fingertips along the words before handing it back to him. He fluidly pocketed the cards and the pen in a gesture she imagined he'd been coached to execute smoothly. "And I know you will be working on several styles with your calligraphy tutor," she said, barely suppressing a smile at the mental image of Kristin laboring to perfect Spenserian script, naked except for her collar and heels. I can't imagine penmanship was something Daddy ever worried about in his slaves, she thought. Remember what her father liked, she suddenly felt awkward and stood up abruptly. "I should show you the rest of... where you will be working." When she opened a side door into her bedroom, Evan rose from the floor and followed her noiselessly into the next room.

"My bedroom," Elaine said, and then fell silent. After a moment, she settled onto a chaise lounge that stood along the windows and had a view of the back gardens. She nodded and Evan followed her. She held out her hand, and he settled on the floor beside her before kissing her palm in supplication. Elaine sighed softly and felt a fluttering in her sex accompanied by a giddy sense of power. Is this ownership? she thought to herself. Is this what it feels like to own a slave of my own?

Evan tilted his head and looked up at her. There was a long silence in the room.

"I know from her notes that Alex—Ms. Selador—has personally ensured that you are able to... that you can handle my particular preferences skillfully," she began, trying to sound confident. "It might be nice..." she trailed off.

He looked at her with raised eyebrows and then at the bed. In response, she slid off the chaise onto the floor beside him and let him return to kissing first her palm and then her elbow and her shoulder. She closed her eyes, opened them, and closed them again. She slid her dress up her thighs and her panties off to accommodate Evan's insistent kissing and touches. She wound up splayed out on the floor, with several pillows from the chaise tucked under her head and hips.

"I think two," she said finally, licking her lips. Evan responded by slipping two fingers into her cunt lips and teasing at the entrance before sliding into her. She was so wet that they went in effortlessly. She sighed happily and rolled her hips up against his hand. "Oh, God yes, that's good," she whispered. "Three."

In response, he added another one. Now she could really feel the thickness of his hands, the width adding up. She gripped her muscles playfully against his hand and he responded by pressing more firmly into her. She spread her legs wider in response and tilted her hips up a bit. In response, his fingertips pushed more firmly against the top of her vagina, making her moan. She inhaled sharply through her teeth. "Mmmhm, yes, exactly, just there. More! I want you to play with my... pinch my nipples," she said breathlessly. With his free hand, Evan reached out and squeezed her nipple tentatively.

"No!" she said, opening her eyes suddenly. She reached up and found one of his nipples under the silk, then pinched it sharply. His mouth opened in a silent gasp of pain. For a moment, his hand stopped moving.

"Exactly!" she panted. "Just. Like. That."

He nodded and pinched her nipple again, this time much more firmly. She threw her head back and ground down onto his hand. "Perfect," she hissed. "Four."

Evan paused to adjust his wrist, adding his little finger to the others and then pressing into Elaine's cunt again. When she tilted her hips slightly to the side, he adjusted the angle of his wrist and curved his fingers up against her, exactly as he'd been coached. With his other hand, he tightened the grip on her nipple.

"Yesyesyesyesyesyesyes," she panted in response. "That, sweet merciful—that." Her voice was still soft, but insistent. "Oh my god—tomorrow, have flowers sent to Ms. Selador with my thanks. Lilacs ... or... vintage... roses..." she said between gasps. "That..." she said again, before arching her back and pressing against his hand one final time. The joint of his thumb rolled against her clit and as she came and then went limp against him.

"I mean it. Flowers," she mumbled dreamily. When she opened her eyes again, Evan was wiping his hand carefully with a handkerchief. Seeing her gaze, he smiled slightly and then looked down before flicking his eyes up to her and raising his eyebrows.

"Yes, I am pleased."

He smiled slightly and looked down at his hands again.

"Next time, we'll do the whole thing," she said, shuddering slightly before sitting up, her back against the front of the chaise. "Would you like a reward?"

He looked up at her, startled.

"You may have a word. Just one."

Evan looked up at her and licked his upper lip. "Ma'am," he whispered solemnly, without looking away.

It was silent between them for several long breaths. "Yes," Elaine said finally. "Good choice."

She pulled herself up onto the chaise and smoothed her dress down. "After that, I'm suddenly hungry. Go downstairs," she began, even as Evan was rising to his feet, "and get a tray for me. I'm sure Cook will have something. Tell them," She stopped short. "Convey to them that I will eat in my room tonight. If you're fast enough, I might let you sit at my feet while I do," she said, trying not to sound too giddy. "Go on!"

Evan grinned at her and slipped out of the room.

"Effective ownership!" Elaine said to the empty room. "I think I'm starting to get the hang of it." She leaned back and began daydreaming about what else she might like to do with her new slave, with the rest of the slaves. When she roused herself out of her reverie, it had gone from late afternoon to early dusk—more than half an hour, certainly.

She started to wonder if Evan had gotten lost on the way to the kitchen. Come to think of it, in the two months that Elaine had been in and out of the house, she didn't think she'd visited the kitchen once. She smoothed her hair back reflexively and got up. She followed the hallway back to the front stairs and then started down them. It was silent in the front of the house. Confused, she retraced her steps and went the other way down the hall, until she found the servants' stairs at the back of the hall.

As Elaine started down the narrow winding stairs, she could hear several voices. By the time she approached the bottom, the voices were louder, and there was laughing. She stopped just short of the last turn of the stairs.

"Hit 'im harder!" she heard a woman's voice shriek. "Oh, but don't leave bruises! If Misssss Elaine Fucking O'Keeffe ever notices anything, she might notice that!"

That was followed by laughter, male and female.

"Here, boy! Come get it!" she heard a male voice say. A low whistling and then more laughter followed it. "Again!"

"If he hollers, let him go!" said another female voice. More laughter. "Eenie meenie miney moe!"

Elaine stepped down the last few stairs and turned the corner into sheer chaos. She was on the edge of the kitchen; the space between what she guessed was the slaves' dining room and the kitchen itself. Inside the kitchen, what must be the entire household staff was gathered around the room. Cook—she could tell by the apron—and several other women were brandishing wooden spoons. Kristin was leaning against a young man wearing a gray coverall who had a leather strap in his hand. On the floor at the center of the group was Evan.

He was down on his hands and knees, his pants pulled down. There were red spoon-shaped marks on his ass and thighs—clearly, someone had been smacking him enough to raise marks. One of the younger women was holding a tray above his head—Elaine assumed it was the tray she'd sent him for.

"What. The. Hell!" Elaine yelled furiously. "What the hell is going on here?"

There was a moment of laughter that died away quickly. "Oh, Miss!" said Kristin, moving towards Elaine and tossing her hair, "You shouldn't be here! This isn't the place for you!"

Other slaves in the room murmured in agreement. "We'll send your new boy back up to you, Miss Elaine," said the man in the gray coverall. "But first, there's hazing—we've all done it."

Kristin had bridged the gap between them and reached out to pat Elaine's arm. "I'm so sorry, Miss—we've made your dinner late. I promise, we'll bring it right up, and your pretty new secretary, too," she said, smiling. "But you can't be here, this isn't your place, you know. Sir—your father—he never came back here."

Elaine's spine went cold with anger. She slapped Kristin hard across the face. "My father is dead." Kristin burst into tears and crumpled to the floor in a half-kneeling position.

There was a sudden sobering silence in the room. All movement stopped.

"My father is dead, and this is my house now. You are my slaves now—or you have no place here at all."

"That's harsh," someone said from a corner of the room.

"You think that's harsh?" Elaine said, looking over the faces in the room. "Harsh will be the letters that go into your files about this behavior. Would you—any of you—like this to be the last contract you ever have in the Marketplace?"

Out of the corner of her eye, she could see Evan getting to his feet and dressing himself. She snapped her fingers and he stepped past everyone to stand near her. She glanced over at him. He tilted his head towards her and let one corner of his mouth turn up in the tiniest of a smile.

"That man—Evan—belongs to me. His contract says I own his voice and every sound he makes. All of the rest of you supposedly belong to me, too—or you have no place in this house. If you don't like it, you may leave tonight. I've reviewed your contracts and my father's will, so I know what your rights are. If I allow you to stay on and I ever catch you attempting to cause him to violate the terms of his contract again, I will release you on the spot. Do you understand me?"

There was silence in the room except for the echo of Elaine's voice in the room.

"Yes, Miss Elaine," Kristin said weakly from floor nearby.

"My father is dead, God bless him. I am the Owner here now. You will call me 'Ma'am' from now on. Do you understand me?"

"Yes, Ma'am," Kristin whispered softly from her crouched position. Elaine paused and held out a hand to her. Kristin took it and rose to her feet shakily.

"Yes, Ma'am," repeated the rest of the slaves assembled in the room.

"Evan is now overdue to bring my dinner tray," Elaine said to the entire room, her voice soft but steel-edged. "I'm going back to my room. Please see this error is corrected, and never repeated." Again she felt that giddy sense of power, but this time it felt like it was settling in to rest, a warm thing curled up against her spine. She paused to look slowly across the room, and then turned and headed back up the winding stairs to her parlor.

Five minutes later, Evan glided into the room with her dinner tray. She motioned to her writing desk and he laid it down for her there. She put the napkin in her lap and reached for the salad fork. He had settled onto the floor next to her, kneeling again, looking up at her through lowered lashes. She couldn't read his expression, couldn't tell what he was thinking. Maybe, she thought, I don't care what he's thinking.

She paused before picking up the fork. "Tomorrow morning at ten, I will begin meeting with them individually to review their contracts and determine who stays. Arrange a schedule for it, starting with senior household positions. A quiet room downstairs with a desk. Have furniture moved if necessary."

This time, she didn't look at him for approval. "Now, you may continue the story," she said, taking up her fork again. She heard him take a deep breath and blow it out slowly.

"The King of the Connacht became angry when he heard his queen's words, and sat up in bed. 'You had money, but I had lands, my queen, and strong brothers, and vassals. You had money, but enemies at your door.' The queen laughed at him, "I had enemies, but now I have none, and you have become a man dependent on a woman's fortune. I am still the greatest between us," Evan began, his voice lightly resonant.

Elaine sighed to herself and took a bite. Effective ownership, she thought again, and smiled to herself as she listened.

Foreword

Sections of the Marketplace books that take place during training are among the most popular scenes. Training is its own fetish, and any excuse to write a sizzling "punishment" scenario will please a certain sort of reader. So, I was surprised to find only one story actually set in the midst of training—but delighted at how different this will feel compared to a standard "bad slave gets a spanking" style of narrative. The Marketplace is home to characters of many sizes, classes, colors, ethnicities, religions, ages, bodies, and identities, united only by their membership in the same shared universe. Finding the secretive world of slaves and trainers and owners is only one step in the continual journey of finding that place where someone fits in. And not every miss-step can be addressed with a flogging.

Sassafras Lowrey is an internationally award-winning storyteller, author, artist, and educator. Most recently ze received an Honorable Mention from the 2011 Astraea Lesbian Writers Fund. Sassafras is the editor of the two-time American Library Association honored and Lambda Literary finalist *Kicked Out* anthology, which brought together the voices of current and former homeless LGBTQ youth. Hir prose has been included in numerous anthologies and magazines. Sassafras regularly lectures and facilitates LGBTQ/Leather storytelling workshops at colleges and conferences across the country. Hir debut novel *Roving Pack* was released autumn 2012, and ze has also edited *Leather Ever After*, an anthology of BDSM fairy tale retellings released by Ravenous Romance. Sassafras lives in Brooklyn with hir Daddy, puppies, and kitties. To learn more about Sassafras and hir work, visit www.SassafrasLowrey.com.

Hiding In Plain Sex
Sassafras Lowrey

It started our first night at the Training House and had become a ritual to take turns telling the story of how we ended up as slaves on this path, in this house, preparing to do something most of the world thought was fantasy or downright insane. The others' stories had gone how Sam had expected, the predictability of the soft-world titleholder who had been spotted at a bar; the one who was intellectually titillated by theories of power exchange in college and then just took it to the next level. Sam mostly stayed silent during story time. Hy wasn't sure they were really supposed to be talking in the first place, but more than that hy dreaded what was coming. Sam had stayed aloof and distant from the other three in his training group and didn't like that hy knew there would be an expectation for hym to share hys story. It wasn't so much that Sam was embarrassed about where hy came from; hy just didn't know how to relate to the fancy soft world conferences they all now mocked so intensely. On the night that was hys turn to share Sam refused, said hy was tired and rolled over.

That night, hys dreams were haunted by the story hy couldn't bring hymself to share with the others. Sam remembered every detail of hys eighteenth birthday; coming home that day to find everything hy owned—cassette tapes, books, childhood toys, and clothes—piled on the sidewalk of hys parents home. With a sinking feeling hys eyes rested on the shoebox filled with letters and photographs from all hys ex-girlfriends. They knew.

Sam tried to open the sassdoor but found hys key didn't work. Hy kicked it hard and heard the steel toe of his boot splinter the corner of the doorjamb, but the door didn't budge. Things had never been easy at hys parent's home but Sam thought hy'd hid the queerness well enough. Kneeling down on the sidewalk Sam emptied hys backpack of schoolbooks and packed everything that would fit—all the boy jeans hy had painstakingly saved up all hys summer job money to buy and a few t-shirts—and started walking.

Sam spent all money hy had that night on entrance to the leather club hy'd seen advertised in the back of the alternative weekly paper.

Hy hadn't thought they would let hym in, being under-age and all, but no one carded and hy slipped into the shadows watching everything hy'd dreamed of come alive before hym. A little after midnight an older dyke approached, introduced herself as AJ and hy followed her to a St. Andrew Cross. Sam had dreamed of this for years, but wasn't about to tell her it was hys first time. Hy braced hymself as hy felt her heavy flogger connect to the soft skin under hys sports bra and across hys back. Again and again hy felt her breaking hym open but hy would not cry. At the end of the night he shook her hand and thanked her. Sam so desperately wanted AJ to invite hym home, but she didn't.

It wasn't until the end of the night when AJ had left with her friends that Sam had to grapple with the reality of being on hys own. That night, hy slept in the bus depot clutching hys backpack and trying to look like hy was waiting to catch a bus. In the morning hy went to the library. Washing up with the sticky pink soap and hard paper towels in the bathroom, hy held back the tears. Hy sat in the abandoned reference section of the library and realized it wasn't even hys parents hy was crying for, but for the loss of what hy'd shared the night before with AJ and was afraid hy wouldn't find again.

Hy panhandled downtown, spinning a story to businessmen and busy mothers with toddlers heading to the greenmarket. Hy told a story about a sick mother at home and a lost bus ticket. Sam tried never to lie, but hy needed to see AJ again. By evening hy had enough for some fast food and entrance to the bar.

AJ seemed to be waiting for hym.

Soon Sam was working odd jobs and panhandling just for admission to the bar. Only in that smoky haze, with AJ, did hy feel safe. Sam spent hys nights in a squat at the edge of the industrial area of downtown. Hy'd met other queer kids like hym and they welcomed hym, but hy stayed distant and never told them where hy spent hys time.

AJ started training hym.

Sam spent hys days in the library studying and writing reports for AJ. As a kid hy'd never spent much time focused on book learning and yet hy excelled in hys studies of proper table settings, tea service, and household management. For some reason the books hy used seemed to never be in high demand and hy was able to check some out for weeks at a time to read by flashlight curled in hys sleeping bag at the squat. AJ expected precise reports of everything hy was learning delivered to her weekly and Sam thrived under the pressure and expectation.

Hy remembered too, the night she pierced hys nipples claiming hym as her own. Hy'd thought hy was home forever; hy left the squat and moved into her small apartment struggling to put into practice everything hy'd learned from the books. Hy thought they were happy together until the day when AJ didn't go to work and told hym they needed to talk.

Sam brought them coffee bracing for the worst, for a breakup that hy didn't know if hy could live through. It was an end, but nothing like hy'd imagined. AJ told him that she had a confession, and her story tumbled out.

She'd once been a slave but in a way far deeper than hy could imagine. AJ told hym about the Marketplace, of her years of service. She had left to take a lover, but her partner had died a few years previously. Unexpectedly, she had taken a shine to Sam, the first person who had really enchanted her; and although she wanted to keep hym to herself, she knew hy needed more than she could give hym.

Sam leaned against the cool bathroom wall grateful for the unexpected solitude. Everyone had been so rude toward him for the last few days—ever since he refused to tell hys story at bedtime. It wasn't until that moment that Sam realized in hys weeks here in training, this was the first time hy had truly been alone. Hy had almost forgotten what privacy felt like; a strange realization for someone who'd spent so much time alone.

On the first day, Chris explained to the group that they were to share the bathroom, and with the limited time to ready themselves for the day they had better help each other. Something as simple as dressing had always been private for hym so Sam had to learn quickly to abandon modesty. Sam remembered that day, how they'd all arrived eager but terrified, the reality sinking in for each of them that they were truly becoming part of the Marketplace. As usual, Sam had mostly kept to hymself, not really bonding with the others and was grateful that on this late afternoon they were all busy with chores or studying, as hy should have been doing.

Sam felt the warm pulsing of deep muscle bruising as hy closed hys eyes and leaned against the cool tile. Hard and wet, Sam swallowed a groan and stood straight, trying desperately to think of anything but the way hys clit throbbed, begging for hys hand to slip into hys pants. Sam let hys mind turn to the way Chris stood over hym; never before had Sam been so grateful for hys shortness. Hys thoughts lingered on the memory of Chris' strap, before painfully shifting to silently reciting the conjugation of French vowels, a skill hy'd recently started trying to learn in hopes of increasing hys usefulness for an owner. Another moment spent lingering on Chris' precision and focus in everything from dress to manners to physical punishment and Sam knew hy would loose all resolve and cum without even so much as taking hys hands from behind hys back where hy'd safely curled them to resist the temptation of hys throbbing clit.

Standing there, Sam realized hy hadn't expected to miss sex so much. It wasn't that hy hadn't known how important it was; it just hadn't occurred to hym it would be taken away. AJ had used hym often, and hy was used to fucking girls at the squat who were always eager for hym to take them. Everything here at the house was harder than Sam thought it would be, and yet despite the exhaustion and strain to learn a new life, hy'd never felt more at home. Hys life had more meaning in the few weeks hy'd spent here in this house. Still, it was so hard to watch when household guests used the others, or even worse when after dinner one of them was chosen to be used by Alexandra or Grendel. Those nights, Sam could hardly concentrate on readying himself for bed, hys focus constantly being pulled to the empty beds in their quarters.

It was no secret that Sam wasn't being used sexually. Everyone noticed, speculating about it in hushed whispers when they thought Sam was far enough away not to hear. Because hy'd never really allowed hymself to bond with them, Sam had mostly been suffering in silence, running fears and scenarios through hys head, convinced that the lack of attention was some kind of homophobic response, an attempt at getting hym to conform to gender norms. Standing in the empty bathroom Sam shook hys head. Everything hy'd ever known about the Marketplace told him it should have been a place that had room for people like hym. God, the second hy'd arrived at the house and seen Chris hy'd known exactly what hy was and the recognition had put Sam a little more at ease entering the house that first day. Yet, it had been weeks without so much as a tweak of hys nipple and hy knew hys grasp of logic was crumbling.

On hys first day Sam had been supplied with a uniform the same has hys male counterparts—simple pants and a shirt. The only difference in hys uniform was the thick elastic compression shirt that hy'd found, folded under a pair of briefs. Sam had been binding hys chest for years and had been a little worried how hy'd handle the dysphoria if that were taken away from hym when hy entered the house. But Sam knew that by becoming a Marketplace slave, comfort was no longer hys concern; the appearance of hys body would be at the sole discretion of his trainers and then owners and hy'd have to handle the dysphoria should they wish to alter hys appearance. But that afternoon, the house had explicitly supported and cultivated hys gender expression. Hadn't they?

Sam knew the others were not prevented from sexual release. To the contrary, Molly, one of the girls in hys group, was supposed to make a regular practice of offering herself to others as some kind of polar opposite punishment to hys. Sam leaned back against the tile wall and let the tears spill from hys eyes. Hy couldn't remember the last time hy was this frustrated, and couldn't understand what hy did wrong, but knew that hy had to do something.

When Sam arrived at dinner that night the others erupted into laughter. Hy wore the plain simple dress the women had grown accustomed to. Hys breasts were embarrassingly perky and the thick steel rings AJ put into hym were as visible as hys hard nipples against the thin fabric. Sam hadn't worn a dress in years. Even as a child hy'd refused anything even remotely feminine and was beaten on more than one occasion for showing up to Sunday school or a family party in dirty overalls. In school Sam had learned to fight, and mostly was left alone. Once hy'd hit the streets hys masculinity became prized. Hy found hys people and they'd clung together. Never in all those years had it occurred to hym that hy'd ever by hys own hand wear anything even remotely feminine. Sam held the tears back as hy entered the kitchen. He was confused, broken, and humiliated.

Hy'd barely made it to hys chair when Chris became visible in the doorway demanding an explanation for the disturbance. Sam was to hys feet before the others but kept hys eyes on his salad plate.

"Sam, with me," was all Chris said and Sam left the room

knowing all the others were watching. Chris led Sam to the library where hy tried to remain calm though the painful silence. There, Chris handed a stack of fabric to Sam; immediately hy recognized it as hys male uniform and binder. With an unmistakable smirk Chris asked, "Did I miss the notice that it was drag night?"

Humiliated, Sam could no longer hold the tears back as hy stripped out of the dress, binding and putting hys pants and shirt on. Ignoring the emotional outburst, Chris calmly requested an explanation for the sudden change of appearance. Sam took a deep breath to control hys voice before stammering about how hy hadn't been used since hys arrival like the others and how hy didn't know why, and all hy could think of was that if hy looked like a woman hy would be wanted. Chris stood in silence while the boi finished. Finally with the precision Sam so admired, he spoke.

"Nothing here is an accident. If someone wanted you to look different, you would know about it. This sort of forced gender experiment is not usually the way this house works. I wouldn't have thought I would have to explain that to you."

"Please forgive me, Chris" Sam stammered before continuing, "May I please ask a question?"

Chris contemplated the request for a moment before nodding.

"If it's not a punishment for my gender then why haven't I been used like the others?" Sam finished, hys eyes tracing the outlines of books on the lowest shelves trying to hold hys voice steady. What followed was an exchange that Sam knew would be branded into hys memory.

"Boy," Chris began "what have you observed about the group of trainees here?"

Sam was confused and uncertain of the right response but knew after hys performance this evening hy needed to answer. "I'm not certain. We've all come from such different places it's hard to compare us," hy finally offered.

"Right. You each took a different path to arrive here at these doors, and you will leave changed, but still different from each other as well. We are here to mold and train you to enter the Marketplace, to teach you the skills that will make you valuable property, but you will not be interchangeable robots." Chris spoke slowly. Sam hung on each word.

"The fastest way to failure is comparing your path to that of another, trying to walk in their shoes and assume their experiences. The key to success is owning where you've come from. Understanding, respecting, and honoring what has brought you here."

Sam could feel the tears burning hot behind hys eyes, threatening to escape. Then, to Sam's surprise, Chris asked hym to recount details of hys sexual experiences. "Tell me," he said. His voice was oddly gentle.

It all came out then; all the women hy'd fucked for a place to stay when the weather turned cold, or whom hy'd let beat and fuck hym senseless on those early nights at the club when hy couldn't find AJ. Words spilled of the people had seen how much hy could take, and how unattached hy was. It had been a sport then, to see if hy could take more, go deeper and further. Sam thought of hys back and how it bore the scars of cuttings hy'd never even known were going to happen. Hy thought of all the people hy'd let fuck hym.

Hy didn't know when the words had stopped.

Suddenly realizing that Chris was silently watching, hy flushed deeply. Tears no longer containable flowed silently down hys cheek as hy spoke. "I think... I understand what you've been trying to teach me," Sam finally stammered.

Chris nodded for hym continue.

Taking a deep breath Sam began, "I've always been good at sex, everyone told me so. I didn't need to get off. I learned to pleasure others, to give them my body, energy, whatever they were looking for, but..." Sam's voice began to shake as hy struggled to form words around this new understanding. "I haven't always been... present in those moments, haven't always really wanted to be there it's just...." Hy trailed off for a moment eyes tracing the edges of books again, trying to compose hymself. Trying to still the tears continuing to fall.

"It's just that sometimes sex was the closest to real surrender I could get... and I took what I could get because I needed it so badly."

When Sam opened hys eyes, Chris was nodding. "The Trainers and I hoped this would help you realize that you no longer need to hide in sex. By entering the Marketplace you've surrendered yourself to a life where you will no longer have to fight to get a taste of what you have spent your lifetime craving. It will not be easy, but you no longer have to seek distilled hints of this life. If you work for it, if you push yourself for it, it is yours. Now, I think you'd best join the others." He took the discarded dress and made a curt motion of dismissal, saying no more.

Sam returned to the dining room at the end of dinner. Hy had expected the others would tease and taunt hym as hy returned more properly attired, with his cheeks tear-stained. Much to hys surprise, everyone held their tongue and finished eating in silence. After dinner and evening chores, Sam returned to the quiet of the library to study until bedtime. As hy passed through a darkened corridor in route to the slaves quarters, hy turned a corner and suddenly Chris was standing before hym. Gasping in surprise Sam lowered hys eyes, but Chris grabbed hys jaw lifting hys face until their eyes met.

"I know what you are. Don't ever front that you're something else. You built yourself, you took care of yourself however you could—so that you would be of value to your future Owners. Don't hide your past. You fought for this, and deserve it as much as anyone else. The Marketplace is your family now; you don't need to hide. You're not the only one who left home early, and there is no shame in where we come from." And then Chris released hym, turned, and walked briskly down the hall the way Sam had come.

Sam slumped against the wall trying to comprehend everything that had just happened before hurrying to the slave dormitory.

And that night when everyone was in bed, Sam surprised them all by apologizing, and at last volunteered to share hys story.

Foreword

From ultra-contemporary, we'll take a step back in time, when the Marketplace operated without the ease of language as clear as the terms sadism and masochism (not yet in common use, and certainly not in the modern "consensual" form) or as esoteric as gender-free pronouns. When a large estate could house a staff from which one could possibly recognize and nurture those whose nature demanded a more intense dynamic than employer and employee could ever supply. It pleased me to leave a staccato tale of rejection and transformation and ease into the story of another orphan of his time, seeking a situation, a purpose, and an identity. From dark, seedy clubs and abandoned buildings to the lush, verdant gardens of a country manor house, two lost and loner foundlings just might find their perfect place.

Over the years, Anna Watson has read and reread the Marketplace books for succor, inspiration, and delight. She is thrilled to find that there's a little corner of the Marketplace world where she can play. For some of her non-Marketplace stories, see *Best Lesbian Erotica 2012*, *Take Me There*; *Best Transgender Erotica*, and *Say Please: Lesbian BDSM Erotica*.

Delirious Moonlight, 1916: Mr. Sloan's Boy
Anna Watson

The grounds were all betwixt and between when Rufus the orphan got a job with Mr. Sloan at Kestrel Point. The bowling green was still just a muddy swath with no grass even seeded yet, and the rhodies were nothing but bits of twigs, their roots tied up in cloth. It was a wonder that the rich people who owned this place weren't worried about their grand plans coming to pass, as muddled as their property looked now, but they didn't seem fussed, the Delacortes. They had the servants set up a table out of doors, right where the patio was to be, and came trooping out for dinner al fresco, with Mr. Sloan as their guest of honor. He was the Landscape Architect in charge of the grounds, and Rufus, working not too far away, could hear the three of them laughing and carrying on. Mr. Sloan was holding forth, waving his hands; "cascade," Rufus could hear him say, "fulfillment" and "panorama"—all of which seemed to please the Delacortes very much.

Rufus wasn't worried about the plans. He had trusted Mr. Sloan on sight, and Mr. Sloan himself was so supremely confident in the importance and beauty of his work that Rufus became so as well. Rufus liked the sketches Mr. Sloan showed him, the certainty with which Mr. Sloan directed him to his tasks. "Dig here," he would say. "Cut down that tree, move this rock," and later, to Rufus's delight, these seemingly unconnected actions would fit into the grand scheme and become a special grove for the Delacortes' as-yet-unborn children, or a secret bower deep in the woods. Very quickly, Rufus signed onto Mr. Sloan's vision, and believed wholeheartedly that the Landscape Architect was on an artistic mission to give the Delacortes a pure reflection of their deepest desires and passions, here on the grounds of their estate. You could almost call it holy. The other laborers complained about the long hours and the filthy temper of their boss, but Rufus loved working with Mr. Sloan. He even liked it when Mr. Sloan took the stuffing out of him if he misunderstood an order and pulled up the wrong plant or dropped a wheelbarrow-full of gravel in the wrong place. When Mr. Sloan lit into him, Rufus stood with his head bowed, not trying to escape the scolding or deny that he deserved it. And it was a strange thing, but it was almost as if he were bathing in the abuse, the harsh words sluicing over him, cleansing him, and when it was over, he was able to get back to work with renewed vigor.

Rufus had been released from the town orphanage that summer when he had turned 18. He would have stayed and worked there, the only home he'd ever known, but there were no openings, or rather, just the one, for a baby nurse, and although Rufus liked babies and would have done his best for them, the Director scoffed, saying it was no job for a man, and he was sent on his way. Luckily it was warm weather, as he spent several nights sleeping rough before he happened to see the notice Mr. Sloan had placed at town hall for laborers. Rufus was the first one there on the appointed day, and because he was tall and brawny, was hired immediately. At first, the work was simply brute labor, cutting down trees, hauling them away, and clearing the land of rocks and brambles. Mr. Sloan, a perfectionist, kept an eagle eye on the laborers, and was not above dismissing one of them for being particularly clumsy. Rufus, a perfectionist in his own right, was soon entrusted with some of the more routine parts of the work. On a good day, Mr. Sloan might give Rufus a few words of faint praise, which would completely go to his head, usually running him right into a mistake, at which point Mr. Sloan would begin a harangue. Nonetheless, Rufus did everything he could to show Mr. Sloan how hard working and trustworthy he was, and was eventually rewarded with a contract through the next summer, with an option to renew.

"The Delacortes are making a very thorough deal of it," Mr. Sloan told him with satisfaction. "Gardens like this could take years to complete."

Years sounded wonderful to Rufus, who had no idea what he would have done if he hadn't gotten this job. He'd had some thought of going to Boston, but he was a country boy at heart, and "fooling around in the dirt and mud," as Cook put it, was the most satisfying thing he'd ever done in his life.

And so the summer passed in active outdoor toil, and when fall came, some of the boys and men working were lost to the harvest, others left for greener pastures in Boston or beyond, but Rufus and a select few stayed on. For them, Mr. Sloan negotiated a deal with the Delacortes, and so Rufus, Jack, Carter, and William were allowed to stay in their room in the servants' quarters, and the estate manager, Mr. Thompson, was told to incorporate them into the household routines.

Rufus was sorry to see the gardens being put to rest, but Mr. Sloan let him know that there was a great deal to be done during the winter, and that along with his household duties and keeping the winter grounds ship shape, he would be taking charge of the greenhouse, the construction of which would be their last outdoor task. There, throughout the cold months, plants carefully chosen in consultation with Mrs. Delacorte would grow up to form an indoor garden of great beauty, one that could be enjoyed in all seasons. In the greenhouse, starting nearer to spring, plants for the grounds would be grown, to be ready for planting once the earth had passed from hard frost. A carpenter was brought in, another stickler for exacting work, and as the days and nights were rapidly growing cooler, the greenhouse was erected with some haste but great care. Mr. Sloan oversaw the construction of the tables and the installation of the trays and lattices on which plants could climb, and when everything was ready, the greenhouse was cozy and weather tight, filled with the aroma of moist, rich soil and the promise of green things growing.

"Now you will see, Rufus," said Mr. Sloan on his last day at Kestrel Point. "Those seeds we planted will soon come nosing up through our good soil, and you will have your work cut out for you. You have my instructions?"

"I do, Mr. Sloan!" Rufus raised the sheaf of papers that Mr. Sloan had entrusted to him, trying to convey with that one gesture how careful he would be and how he would respond to the written instruction with as much good cheer and care as he did to Mr. Sloan's instruction when present. Mr. Sloan nodded and left with no further word.

After watching Mr. Sloan's beat up Ford Runabout carry him away from Kestrel Point—standing at attention until it was out of sight—Rufus did not crumple to the ground with sheer loss, as his heart urged him to do. Instead, he carefully stowed the packet of instructions in a safe, dry spot near the door of the greenhouse, and went about the business of damping down the trays of seeds, carefully, meticulously, with great concentration. It helped him to imagine that Mr. Sloan might burst back in at any moment, and it wouldn't do to be caught in slipshod work.

Rufus and the other boys helped prepare the house for winter, and Rufus stood in the driveway with the rest as Mr. and Mrs. Delacorte motored off for their home in Boston where they would pass the season. That evening after supper, Mabel, the scullery maid, came to fetch him where he was working in the greenhouse. She stood demurely right inside the door, her cheeks very pink from the chill.

"Don't touch anything!" Rufus ordered. His tone was harsher than he had meant, but Mabel didn't complain.

"You've got to report to Mr. Thompson right away," she said. When Rufus began to swipe at the dirt on his clothes, Mabel smiled. "Let me, Rufus. I brought the brush."

Rufus had wondered what she was carrying in a cloth sack, hoping maybe Cook had sent out some biscuits for him. He was always hungry; in that sense, nothing at all had changed from the orphanage, where mealtimes had been too few and far between, with never enough on his plate. In every other way, however, his life had improved immeasurably. Hearing that the estate manager wanted to see him, he felt the bottom of his stomach drop out, and desperately cast his thoughts back over the past few days to see if he'd made a mistake or otherwise been remiss. Careful not to let his emotions show on his face, he submitted to the efficient brushing Mabel gave his clothing, and followed her to the scullery where he washed his hands and face before knocking softly on Mr. Thompson's door.

"Yes, Rufus. Please enter."

Mr. Thompson occupied a small room off the servants dining hall, where he kept a roll top desk for his papers.

"You wanted to see me, Sir?" Rufus stepped inside, closing the door at the older man's gesture.

"Yes, that's right." A disconcerting silence followed, as Mr. Thompson finished writing something in a book, put his pen away, checked the time on his pocket watch, and finally turned his gaze to Rufus. "Comfortable upstairs?" he asked, then, speaking over Rufus's, "Yes, Sir!" said, "Mr. Sloan has given me a good report on you, Rufus. He says you're a good boy, trustworthy and hard working. You know that Mr. and Mrs. Delacorte would never have hired you if not for his recommendation; you are, in a sense, an ambassador for Mr. Sloan in this house."

Rufus stood up straighter. Mr. Thompson leaned forward and continued, "Before he left for Boston, Mr. Sloan told me I could trust you if I needed anything, and I do need something now, Rufus. The other three fellows, William, Carter, and Jack—they're not quite the same caliber as yourself, so Mr. Sloan gave me to believe, and after observing them for these past few weeks, I am inclined to agree. Here's my situation, Rufus: this is a decent house, and we want decent behavior from all of our people at all times. I'm afraid that things are not always entirely decent up in your room, isn't that so?"

Blushing, Rufus thought of the twists of paper he put in his ears every night to stop himself hearing the rough talk of the other three boys. Mr. Thompson's gaze sharpened. "What is it, boy?"

"I," Rufus began. "I..."

"Speak up!" The older man's voice now had a silky, snaky quality that fascinated Rufus, nailing him to the spot.

"I think, I mean, my ears, Sir," Rufus mumbled, repeating himself more clearly when Mr. Thompson once more rapped out, "Speak up!"

"What about your ears?" Mr. Thompson's gaze never left him, and Rufus felt as hooked as a fish on a line. No matter how embarrassing, he knew he would have to confess. Mr. Sloan would require it. The truth was, he hated the way the boys talked about women. He never joined in, and he always felt uncomfortable; because of this, the others accused him of having "lord and lady" manners, of being a mama's boy (a particularly cruel insult in his case), and let him know, with great jollification on their part, that the kind of manners he had could mean only one thing: that he had never had a woman. This was true.

"I stop them up, Sir," Rufus managed to get out, shifting his weight from one foot to another in discomfort. "The others can be so loud and rough, Sir. It keeps me awake at night."

There was a quick flash of humor in Mr. Thompson's eyes and his lips twitched once before his expression sobered again. "I understand. And that is exactly the sort of thing I'm talking about. Mr. and Mrs. Delacorte have entrusted me to make sure that decorum is observed here at Kestrel Point, both in public and in private. As someone who answers directly to Mr. Sloan, do you understand what I'm speaking of, Rufus?"

Rufus didn't know where to look. Of course, he had heard the others getting raucous after sneaking in some liquor; well, they could be raucous even without the liquor, always egging each other on to cast aspersions on one girl or another. Certainly, what went on in their room could hardly be termed decorous. That was why he started blocking them out in the first place.

"I, well, I believe I understand, Sir."

"Good. I'm not asking you to mention anything to them— leave that to me—but I will be counting on you to give me a thorough report when I next send for you. That will be all."

Rufus was on the other side of the closed door before he knew what had happened, before he could ask Mr. Thompson to please be more specific, to give him more detailed instruction. As he stood there trying to collect himself, the housekeeper, Mrs. Regan, appeared. She told him to get back to the greenhouse, then knocked on Mr. Thompson's door and entered.

As he walked rapidly away, Rufus heard her ask, "How did it go, Tommie?" and Mr. Thompson replied, "Oh, yes, he'll do very well," and, uncharacteristically, began to laugh.

That night, Rufus washed and prepared for bed still feeling bewildered. At the orphanage, he had stayed as far away as possible from the boys and girls who tried to curry favor with the Director by reporting on crimes, major and minor, of the other orphans. Rufus had never wanted to turn in other children, even when they did something he didn't approve of, like stealing from each other or from the shops in town. He knew that in the code of manhood, ratting on your companions was just the same as being a traitor, a Benedict Arnold. Yet here was Mr. Thompson asking him to report on his roommates—not just Mr. Thompson, but Mr. and Mrs. Delacorte, and even Mr. Sloan himself. Well, then. If it was for Mr. Sloan, if Mr. Sloan was asking him to unstop his ears and listen in on the rude talk of the other boys, then he would do it. And tell Mr. Thompson all they said and did? Yes. Yes, he would.

When Rufus was 10 and 11, he'd had a bosom buddy at the orphanage. Mikey was a harum-scarum boy with freckles, a sweet smile, and friendly, trusting eyes, despite the hard blows life had dealt him. He and Rufus were together all the time, and when Haley's came by, they stood with the rest of the orphans on a hill in the town park, holding hands as that great comet glimmered and glowed in the sky. "We'll see it again when it next passes by!" they told each other, not in the least able to imagine being over 80 years old, but such was the current of love between them. They never doubted they would remain friends. Not too long after, however, Mikey was adopted by a family moving west, and although he said he would write, Rufus never heard from him again. After that, Rufus kept to himself, though the other children called him stuck up. Here at Kestrel Point, it was no different. At the beginning of the summer, the rest of the crew had attempted to include him in their conversations and pranks, but soon came to see that he was a loner. They mostly came to accept it, and usually left him to his own devices.

He had nothing against the other three, it's just they inhabited another world entirely: they had families and sweethearts and plans for the future, while Rufus had nothing, save now for this work. He liked gardening and was becoming skilled at working with green and growing things. Mr. Sloan once said that Rufus would surely be able to find a place as a gardener at some estate or other after he finished the work at Kestrel Point, that he, Mr. Sloan, would give him a good reference. Rufus had thanked him, but remained hopeful that he might keep working for Mr. Sloan instead, on the next job and the next.

Settling into his single bed, which he had pushed as far from the others as possible, Rufus reached for his twists and ducked his head under the covers, pretending to put them in. He usually fell right asleep, tired from his work, but tonight he remained alert.

"He's down, is he?" This was William. Rufus watched him through near-closed eyes as he flung down a towel with which he'd done a rather indifferent job of washing his face and neck. William was a slovenly, stick-thin fellow, whose looks belied the fact that he was extremely strong and hard working when given a specific task. He also claimed to be extremely well loved by the ladies because of his sizable tackle, and he wasn't shy to show it off to his roommates, either. Tonight, stretched out on his bed, cupping his equipment affectionately, he said, "Oh, that Mabel, she was doing it again tonight!"

"You're a lying pig," said Carter, his red hair standing on end from the vigorous rubbing he'd just given it with a wet towel. He was as neat as William was mussed, prissy almost, and only escaped being called a lady-boy by the fact he'd gotten more than one girl in trouble, and was currently sneaking around with one of the daughters of the richest family in town.

"A lying, desperate pig," agreed Jack, a wiry, dark boy, who was stripping quickly in the chill air, preparatory to sliding between the covers. He always slept completely nude, claiming that ancient Greek athletes in training for the Olympics always slept so. Jack had won many amateur wrestling matches and harbored hopes he would one day be discovered by an impresario and embark upon a marvelous wrestling career.

"Oh, is that right? Then why did she wiggle her sweet ass at me as she passed me in the hall, and why did she reach out for a nice feel of this big fella?" William rubbed himself through his dingy underthings, giving himself the beginnings of an erection.

Rufus held himself very still. He wasn't put off so much by William fondling himself—that he'd seen before—but what he'd said about Mabel was shocking. Hadn't Mr. Thompson made it very clear that there was to be no indecorous behavior in this house? And he had never seen Mabel be anything other than proper. Was this the type of thing Mr. Thompson wanted him to report?

A week later, when Mr. Sloan's seedlings were pushing through the dirt like a pale green rug, Mabel came for Rufus again. "Mr. Thompson wants you," she said, and like before, she brushed him down thoroughly. Did she linger at his backside? Rufus, thinking of everything William had said about her these past few days, pulled away. "That's enough," he said gruffly, hoping he wasn't blushing. She smiled.

"You look presentable now," she said, and led the way back to the main house.

Mrs. Regan was standing beside Mr. Thompson's desk when Rufus arrived. The room was so small that there were barely two feet between him and them, and the proximity of these commanding older staff members began to make Rufus sweat.

"Well?"

"Yes, Sir. Ma'am." Rufus looked down, so embarrassed his ears felt as if they were radiating heat. Mrs. Regan reached out and tweaked one of them.

"Look up when you give your report, boy. Stand straight, arms loose at your sides, hand relaxed. Whatever you do, don't fidget or put your hands in your pockets."

Obeying her exactly, Rufus began to feel surer of himself. Mr. Thompson shifted in his chair and Rufus glanced over at him. Something hard pressed against his cheek, and, startled, he turned back to Mrs. Regan who had acquired a ruler from Mr. Thompson's desk and was adjusting his head with it.

"When you deliver a report, Rufus, you must not look into our eyes, but instead direct a neutral gaze between the two of us, choosing a fixed point on which to focus, such as, perhaps, this clock." She tapped his cheek again, and then tapped the glass dome of a small clock on the desk. Rufus stared at it, his heart beating hard. Another tap of the ruler. He looked pleadingly at Mrs. Regan, and she frowned. "When I instruct you, Rufus, you must offer your thanks."

"Thank you, Ma'am!" he managed.

"You're welcome. Now please give us your report."

"Yes, Ma'am!" Rufus stared desperately at the clock, but it took another tap of the ruler, this time on his other cheek, before he could bring himself to say anything.

"Sir, Ma'am, William keeps speaking poorly of Mabel," he finally blurted out, his voice small and reedy.

"Yes, I suppose he would," Mr. Thompson said. "Go on."

Rufus cleared his throat and was relieved to hear the next words come out at the usual, much lower register. "And both Carter and Jack have taken bread from the kitchen, and..."

"No, Rufus," Mrs. Regan interrupted swiftly. "We don't need to know what hungry young men do to keep themselves fed. You must stick to the subject."

Confused, Rufus ran through the list of faults he'd gathered over the past few days. So many of them had to do with stealing food that he wasn't sure he'd have much more to say. Still, he forged ahead. "Ah, well, Jack and Carter have neither of them gotten a chance to see their sweethearts for almost two weeks now, and they are always going on about being, um, wanting for it, Sir, Ma'am—is this what you want me to tell you?"

Moving his gaze from the clock, Rufus caught a look shared between Mr. Thompson and Mrs. Regan, one he couldn't readily interpret, but which seemed smug and satisfied on the part of Mrs. Regan and predatory on the part of Mr. Thompson. For a moment, Rufus felt light-headed, and he put a hand on the desk to steady himself. Quick as anything, Mrs. Regan swatted it, hard, with the ruler. "Don't touch! Yes, Rufus, this is the information we require from you. Continue."

Sweating, Rufus recounted how Jack had been talking about the ancient Greeks, how he'd been studying their practices, and learned that warriors had noble and manly friendships with fellow warriors or younger men. That their love was pure, untainted with womanly concerns and foolishness, how, he, Jack, so admired the purity of this ancient culture.

"He's been sneaking into our library, it sounds like," murmured Mr. Thompson, a hint of admiration in his tone. "And how did the other boys take this interesting information?"

Rufus blushed. "William fell asleep Sir, in the middle of Jack's lecture, but Carter liked to hear it, Sir, and he, they..."

"Speak smoothly, Rufus, and finish your sentences. It's impolite to make us wait."

"Yes, Ma'am, I'm sorry." Rufus hardly knew where he was or what was happening any more. Normally shy and reticent in his speech, he didn't quite understand why it was he found himself in this small, close study, speaking of such private things, things he'd tried to ignore, the animal behavior of his less couth fellow workers, the things they got up to that he found sordid and unpleasant. Daring a very brief glance again at the two senior staff members, however, the expressions on their faces spurred him on, comforted him, made him feel that he was in exactly the right place doing exactly the right thing. The avid look in their eyes awoke something in him, as well, and to his horror and embarrassment, he felt his own penis stir as he laid out in detail exactly how Jack and Carter had honored the ancient Greeks last night.

Back in the greenhouse, Rufus did something he had never done before, something that never would have occurred to him but now seemed the best thing to do, the only thing to do. The idea had come to him, so strong, so clear, to unite with the soil, the good, rich element. Checking to make sure he was truly alone, he undid his trousers and removed his penis, stiff and throbbing since making his report to Mr. Thompson and Mrs. Regan (something they surely must have noticed but had been polite enough not to mention). There was a barrel of good, dark earth, richly composted and ready to be used for planting, that spilled its bounty in the corner of the greenhouse, waiting to be used in Mr. Sloan's grand design. Hurrying now, desperate to get on with it, not able to wait any longer, Rufus upended a jug of water into the barrel and scooped up a handful of the resulting mud. He smoothed it over his penis, falling to his knees, pumping into the slick muck until he was spent. Filthy, panting, he lay curled next to the barrel, bits of sod trickling down onto him. What was it that made him murmur just then, "Thank you, Mr. Sloan?"

Winter came, with gales and snow. The lake froze over and Jack enlisted the boys' help to clear a space for skating. A small shack was dragged out for ice fishing, something Rufus became good at under the tutelage of Evan, the houseman. Always, Rufus kept control of the work in the greenhouse, following Mr. Sloan's instructions carefully, enlisting the help of others when needed.

He found that when he was working for Mr. Sloan, even when Mr. Sloan was not actually present, he became quite bossy, something the other boys resented him for but which Mr. Thompson noticed and approved.

"You're showing yourself to be worthy of your master," he said to Rufus one day, after inspecting the greenhouse and finding everything in excellent order. "I think he would be proud now, to call you his boy."

Mr. Sloan's boy! Although Rufus was accustomed to thinking of himself as no longer a child in any sense of the word except perhaps one—the subject about which he was also teased quite mercilessly by his more experienced roommates—the words rang good and true.

Throughout the winter, as the plants in the greenhouse garden pushed out fronds and buds, Mr. Thompson and Mrs. Regan continued to summon Rufus for reports. Mabel would appear at the greenhouse door, and Rufus would submit to her brushing, a routine that never varied. Then he would follow her to Mr. Thompson's room, gathering himself, collecting his thoughts. After that first, strange and awkward encounter, Rufus became accustomed to his duties, and did his best to accommodate the senior staff's unfathomable desire to hear about the bedroom talk and activities of William, Carter, and Jack. Mr. Thompson and Mrs. Regan offered Rufus vocabulary where his own failed, and slowly, they began to draw him out concerning his own thoughts.

"Now Rufus, when Carter parted himself for Jack," Mr. Thompson said after Rufus had reported, once more, on Jack's and Carter's Athenian exploits, "how did you yourself feel?"

"Feel, Sir?" Rufus's member leapt in his trousers as Mr. Thompson spoke of feeling, of parting. He closed his eyes briefly and again saw Carter, lying on his back, legs up in the air, his hands eagerly holding himself open as Jack knelt up, stroking himself to splendor. Until this moment, Mr. Thompson and Mrs. Regan had never mentioned Rufus's quite obvious tumescence when he gave his report; it seemed that as long as he kept his eyes on the clock and his posture as they required, his words would be heard and his condition ignored.

"Feel." Mrs. Regan employed her ruler, not gently, and not on his cheek. It hurt. It felt wonderful. Rufus yelped, then felt Mr. Thompson's hand come across his mouth.

"You will be silent," the older man said in his ear. Rufus sagged against his strong arm for just a moment, then stood up straight again. "Good," said Mr. Thompson, releasing him. "Mrs. Regan asked you a question."

"Yes, Sir." Rufus hesitated only a moment. Despite his shame, he knew from their previous training that they expected him to speak up and to be sharp about it. "I felt warm, Sir and Ma'am. I felt tricky and tickly down there."

At the words "down there" Mr. Thompson and Mrs. Regan both drew in disapproving breaths.

"Cock, I mean, I'm sorry! My cock stood up at attention, Sir, Ma'am, and was clamoring for a stroke."

"Better. And did you? Give yourself a stroke?"

Rufus was not accustomed to reporting on his own activity, which had become more and more creative over the past few months and which now included other forms of release apart from good, honest soil, although his lewd activities were still solitary. Rufus again hesitated, and again felt the stinging slap of the ruler against his instrument.

"Yes, Sir, Ma'am, I did stroke! All the while that Jack was giving it to Carter and William was snoring away, I pulled at my own balls and gave myself strokes and strokes!"

"And when you jettisoned, my poor, wanting Rufus, whose name did you groan into your pillow, I wonder?" Mrs. Regan was now running her ruler up and down Rufus's cock, the hard edge rasping across the material of his trousers. Since it wasn't a direct question, however, Rufus thought perhaps he needn't answer, and, happily, neither Mr. Thompson nor Mrs. Regan seemed to require the information. Perhaps they already knew.

About the time the ice began breaking up on the lake, Mr. Thompson and Mrs. Regan gathered the staff together to announce that Mr. and Mrs. Delacorte would be returning to Kestrel Point, and soon thereafter would be hosting a party to welcome Mr. Sloan back to continue work on the grounds. There were other details, but Rufus had stopped listening when he'd heard the name of his master. Was he ready? Was the greenhouse ready? He could hardly bear to wait until they had been dismissed to run out there, go over and over his instruction booklet, now somewhat the worse for wear. The temperature in the greenhouse was just right and the panes of glass ran with nourishing moisture, the garden had grown up as Mr. Sloan had directed, the plants flourishing, and the whole place looked and smelled deliciously fecund. Mr. Sloan would certainly find that everything was as it should be.

Then there was no time to fret, although Rufus continued to check on the greenhouse every free moment he had. Over the next week, the house was turned out from top to bottom, and the boys were kept busy lifting, beating rugs, rearranging, lugging boxes and cases from delivery wagons to kitchen; all manner of other physical tasks. Although Mr. Thompson and Mrs. Regan lost their tempers a hundred times a day, spirits were high, as the staff was fond of Mr. and Mrs. Delacorte, and after the long, quiet winter, ready for some excitement. When at last the Delacortes' car made its appearance on the drive, Rufus stood with the rest of the staff, barely remarking that Mrs. Delacorte was indeed expecting, as Mabel had whispered to him. He was waiting for a beloved figure who apparently had not made his way down from Boston with the Delacortes after all.

The Delacortes immediately secluded themselves in the drawing room with Mr. Thompson and Mrs. Regan to receive their household reports, and Rufus continued to be kept busy. He knew now that the event in several days time was to be a May Day celebration, although he had also overheard Mrs. Regan say something about Beltane, a word he didn't know. He helped erect a May Pole and made sure there was enough dry wood and kindling for the bonfire. Still no Mr. Sloan, and Rufus thought he would burst from waiting. The day of the party, Mabel brought him an oatcake, still warm from the oven, and tried to get him to speculate with her about the guests who had begun arriving, but there was only one person Rufus wanted to see.

Near midnight, Rufus made his escape from tending the bonfire and started for the greenhouse. He had been on alert the entire evening, but Mr. Sloan had not appeared, and Rufus was beginning to give up hope. The party had grown more and more crowded with wildly costumed guests running everywhere as the consumption of spirits increased, and Rufus had been called on to serve food, wash up, tend the fire, just anything the nearest person could use him for. Prescribed duties seemed to be suspended for the party, and he even saw Mrs. Regan laughing and throwing armfuls of wood onto the bonfire that was crackling and leaping on the shores of the lake. Mr. Thompson, last he saw, was rosy faced, up to his elbows in sudsy water in the scullery, while Mabel, who had found a colorful scarf somewhere, danced and sang behind him, her hair tied up like a gypsy. As Rufus made his way through the crowd, hands reached out to tweak his bum, people bumped into him on purpose, and one masked woman stopped him in his tracks by sweeping up his shirt and placing her lipsticked mouth on one nipple for a long suck while her sharp-nailed fingers diddled the other. When she came up for air, she smacked his belly and moved off, leaving him weak-kneed and erect. He thought immediately of his barrel of earth, and continued to hurry in that direction.

A creature of habit, Rufus followed a strict routine before allowing himself release. First, he checked the notebook and made sure he had followed the instructions for that day. He took his pitcher of water and wetted down any beds that needed it, and then he thinned the seedlings and performed any other tasks that needed doing. Finally, he swept up. After checking to see that he was alone, he was free to make his way to the barrel. Tonight, he worried that errant guests might stumble into the greenhouse, which did not lock—he had passed people trysting in the woods on his way here—but it was quiet, and he was alone. He had just undone his trousers and was kneeling, preparing his mud, when he heard the door open. If he was very still, there in the shadowy corner, perhaps the person would head back to the more lively area of the party. But now, whoever it was closed the door and began to walk down the middle aisle. Quickly trying to stuff himself back in and make himself decent, Rufus began to rise, when a hand pressed firmly down on his shoulder.

"Don't stop," a light, tenor voice ordered. "I'm quite curious to see how it is you've been tending to my greenhouse."

Rufus gasped and dropped heavily back to the ground, leaning forward so that his forehead rested on the barrel. Mr. Sloan would send him packing, dismiss him for indecorous behavior in the extreme, denounce him to the world as disgusting and coarse. Worse—he would lose any respect he'd ever had for him. His now-limp member still dangling from his open trousers, Rufus began to weep.

"Rufus." The word was like a slap. "I told you not to stop."

Rufus quieted. He could hear the distant noises of the party, shouts and laughter, breaking glass, firecrackers going off, and the splash of some unfortunate taking a spill into the still-frigid lake. His skin vibrated with the nearness of Mr. Sloan, but he didn't dare look up. His cock had regained its vigor at the sound of Mr. Sloan's command. Mr. Sloan shifted his weight and cleared his throat, but before he need issue another order, Rufus got to his knees. Though more agitated than perhaps ever in his life, Rufus continued to prepare his mud, his hand trembling and trembling. Tentatively, he began to stroke himself so that soon his cock was slick with mud. He went slowly, unsure, until Mr. Sloan urged him to go faster.

As Mr. Sloan issued further commands, Rufus did more. He smeared mud over his chest and fingered his nipples until they stood out, sore and erect; he winkled his filthy finger into his hole, stretched, moaned, and licked his lips. Rufus had always been a shy boy, a boy who kept to himself, and in a very distant part of his mind, he marveled that here he was, acting like a whore, gyrating and vocalizing his horny pleasure before his master.

But he liked it, and he treasured it, and he knew he was doing it right because Mr. Sloan told him he was, and Mr. Sloan was making his own small sounds of pleasure and now Mr. Sloan was undoing the buckle of his belt. Rufus closed his eyes and bent over, offering up his loam-smeared arse, holding himself apart the way he was sure Mr. Sloan would require. Rufus was very inexperienced and had never, ever acted this way in the past, not with man or woman, but he knew what to do now, of course he did because it was true, as Mr. Thompson had told him, it was true, true as his master embraced him around the waist and entered his virgin hole and Rufus cried out and he spasmed and he pushed back against the warm flesh that joined with his. He was. He was now and he would be forever. "Who is my boy?" asked Mr. Sloan, and they both knew the answer.

I want all my places to seem the homes of children and lovers. I want them to be comfortable and if possible slightly mysterious by day, with vistas and compositions appealing to the painter. I want them to be delirious by moonlight... I believe that there is no beauty without ugliness and that it should not be otherwise. Both are capable of stinging us to live. Contrast is more true to me than undeviating smugness. The chief vice in gardens is... to be merely pretty.

—Prescott Sloan

Foreword

Spotters are the major link the Marketplace has between the outside world—kinky or not—and the more rarefied community of their hidden shadow world. They hunt for potential slaves (and potential trainers and owners as well, but those will be stories for another time) and bring them gently into understanding with many varied forms of seduction. With the ability to move between worlds and the responsibility to hold sacred the nature of the Marketplace, they need to be consummate players of all sorts of games—capable of seeing latent skill and coaxing it along and then turning to manage an experienced Marketplace slave or report to a persnickety trainer. That some spotters are also owners or slaves and occasionally trainers is established in the books; I was happy to see more on their precarious balancing act turn up in a story about risk and consequences.

Jamie Thorsen is a gleefully sadistic polyamorous thirty-something dominant currently living in Atlanta, GA. When he's not committing acts of torture and depravity on surprisingly enthusiastic victims, he's attending Burning Man-type events, herding cats, co-leading Team Bad Idea (an Atlanta TNG kink social group), and working on his first novel. You can find him on Fetlife as "Poeticmotion" or reach him at poeticdominance@gmail.com.

Pearls in the Deep Blue Sea
Jamie Thorsen

"For spotters who operate in the soft world, the explosive growth of the kink community and the advent of Kinkynet have created new opportunities, but also new challenges. We must sift through ever increasing numbers of dilettantes and fetishists to find those who are both suitable for and interested in what the Marketplace has to offer; we must open a thousand oysters to find each pearl. Kinkynet has fostered new levels of connectivity that render the Marketplace ever more vulnerable to exposure and make it even more crucial that spotters carefully vet potential clients.

Despite the difficulties, we've maintained a high level of quality and a steady flow of new clients to the auction block. The ocean into which we dive is deeper and broader than ever before, but the results are worth it; we keep diving, in search of pearls in the deep blue sea."

—From *Diving for Pearls: Spotting in the Social Media Era*

Presentation given at the Academy, by Quentin Yardley and Marie Salazon.

Marie fought back a yawn and leaned against the wall, watching the ebb and flow of movement in the crowded dungeon. She scanned the crowd and resisted the urge to check her watch. Jack would be here sooner or later to relieve her as dungeon monitor whenever Quentin, her owner, decided he needed her to be somewhere else.

It had been her idea to throw a monthly play party for the local BDSM community at Quentin's fifteen-acre estate just outside of the city. He had been pleased with the success of her idea. She knew that he viewed most of these people as vulgar dilettantes, and she couldn't argue, but the events served their purpose of keeping the household connected to the local community.

The door to the outside terrace opened; her friend and protégé, Kitten, stepped through it and scowled at the crowded dungeon. Her red hair cascaded down to frame a porcelain face that was spattered with freckles; her tiny stature made her appear fifteen instead of twenty-two. She tried to look fierce; knee-high spiked boots and torn fishnets stretched up underneath her black microskirt, a Tank Girl graphic was emblazoned across her stretchy top, and an army surplus medic bag hung from her shoulder as a purse. Like her namesake, though, her claws weren't enough to keep people from calling her adorable.

Marie, curious as to why Kitten looked so upset, followed a few feet behind the girl as she navigated the dungeon, heading toward the back corner. Kitten's fiancé Danny stood in front of a girl suspended in a web of saran wrap, holding a Hitachi vibrator to her clit. Another woman carefully sliced a square out of the saran wrap over one breast. The nipple clamps hanging from her belt telegraphed her plans.

From ten feet away, Marie couldn't make out the conversation. They exchanged some words, Danny pointed at his backpack, and Kitten retrieved a set of keys from it. She stepped closer to Danny and tilted her head up; without flipping off the vibrator, he leaned down, brushed his lips against hers, and returned his focus to the suspended girl. Kitten shook her head, turned her back, and began pushing her way back through the crowd, headed for the door of the dungeon.

Marie caught up to Kitten and reached out, grabbing her shoulder. "You okay, girl?"

Kitten embraced Marie tightly. It took her half a minute to let go. "Can we talk?" she asked, hope in her voice.

"Sure, sweetie. I'm DM right now, so you'll need to go find my owner and see if anyone can take over for me."

"I can do that. I picked up a bottle of wine from the gas station on the way here. I'm going to grab it and smoke a cigarette first. Okay?"

"That's fine," Marie said.

A high-pitched shriek emanated from the back corner; Kitten glanced over her shoulder. "That's what nipple clamps feel like, bitch," she muttered and walked away.

Marie frowned at the venom in Kitten's words. She knew why the girl was acting out. She knew that others viewed Kitten as an immature and often petulant bottom, but she saw the potential in her for so much more. Marie looked at Kitten and saw the elements that, with training, could be molded into a content and obedient slave.

They ended up in the third story alcove, used as a closet for fetishwear. Marie and Kitten sat on the floor underneath a shelf lined with corsets and hoods, the bottle of cheap moscato between them.

Kitten took a long drink straight from the bottle, ignoring the wineglass Marie had brought with her. "I'm just frustrated, that's all," she said.

"That sounded dangerously close to whiny. You're engaged to Danny. If he's staying within the boundaries you've agreed upon, then you need to either renegotiate those boundaries or accept things the way that they are. Passive aggressive bitching won't solve anything."

"He's good to me," Kitten said after a pause. "I just want something more. When we play, it's great, but when playtime is over, the d/s just seems to fade away, and when we go to play parties, he always gets distracted by someone new and shiny."

"From my understanding of your rules, you can play with others too," Marie said.

"With his permission, but it doesn't feel right. If he gave me to someone else, that'd be one thing, because it's... I don't know..."

"An extension of him?"

"Yes! Exactly. Just playing with someone else, it's nice but it's like masturbation, fun but empty. I want to give myself to the person that owns me or the people they choose," Kitten drank from the bottle. "Are you sure you don't want some wine?"

"My master wouldn't like it." They sat in companionable silence for a minute. "Are you in love with him?"

Kitten's face betrayed the flickering thoughts behind her eyes. She was a dreamer, but in a serious conversation, she would turn thoughts around like a Rubik's cube in her brain. It reminded Marie of herself.

"Damn," Kitten gulped down more wine. "Three months ago, when he proposed to me, there wasn't a doubt in my mind. Now... God, I don't know. He swept me off my feet, my first real dom. When he asked me to marry him, of course I said yes. I have everything I wanted. I have a man who takes care of me, loves me, and is as kinky as I am. So why do I freak out about spending the rest of my life with him?"

Kitten shifted into the center of the beam of sunlight from the alcove window; Marie smiled, thinking how much the girl resembled her nickname. "I look at how devoted you and Jack and Gary are to Quentin, how content you are in your service, how proud, how... secure. It's like a whole different level from the rest of us. Danny talks a big game, but when we're not scening, he's just my fiancé. I don't feel owned anymore. I wonder if I ever truly did."

Marie framed her next statement carefully, unwilling to lie but unable to tell the whole truth. "Sweetie, we've all been doing this for years, apart and together. We've learned by trial and error how to make this work."

"It's not just that. It's...I try to anticipate his needs. I try to do the little things. Try to get him to notice my service...no, that's not right. He doesn't have to notice, but...I'm fucking this all up," she said in anguish. "I find myself acting out, breaking the rules just so he'll beat me and I can feel owned again. It's wrong but I just want to know I'm his and sometimes he doesn't even notice and even when he does and beats me, it never lasts!"

"Kitten, at heart, you're a slave." Marie reached out and caressed the younger girl's face. "You have the drive to service. You want structure, someone to provide the framework you need to make the world make sense."

"All I've wanted since I was a little girl was someone to belong to," Kitten said after a pause. "When I first discovered Kinkynet, it was an epiphany. I wasn't some sort of anti-feminist freak. I met Sir and it was like a fairy tale. I cried when he collared me. I felt so proud to be his, like there was nothing I couldn't do.

"But it's not enough. I want to really be owned, like you are. I don't want this to end at the bedroom door. I don't want this to be a game. I mean, I'm smart enough to know that at some level that all of this is a game, but I don't want it to be. I want to be subject to the bidding of my owner, like that stupid Anais Nin quote that's on half the profiles on Kinkynet."

"But do you want someone to really own you or a lover who plays the role?"

"Well," Kitten said. "Wow. That's... I hadn't thought of it like that before."

"You have the fairy tale. You say it's not enough. If you want to be happy, you need to figure out what you want." Marie watched the younger woman, wondering how much of the truth she could reveal. This girl was so much like she had once been, trying to find out where she belonged in the world. Marie knew the answer to Kitten's question, but her fingers searched out her own collar; it reminded her that she was only allowed to say so much. "What if you could become a slave, put up on the auction block, sold to the highest bidder and truly owned?"

Kitten pulled her lighter out of her pocket and toyed with it aimlessly. "Not just the daydream of some sexy hunk of man-meat buying me and carrying me away, but anyone who could write a check?"

Marie smiled at the girl's clarification. "Yes. But someone that would give you that structure, allow you to serve."

Kitten stood up and paced across the room, bringing the bottle with her. She ended up at the window, where she could see the party-goers circulating on the terrace below. Marie simply waited, thinking that if Kitten had claws, she'd be kneading the carpet by now.

"I want to say no," Kitten finally said. "It runs against what I've always told myself about coexisting as a feminist and a submissive, about doing this by choice. But at the same time, if it was my choice, if it was a decision made from strength, that might... that would be different."

"I went through a similar thought process eight years ago. You remind me of myself so much it scares me. Kitten, there's something I've been thinking about for a while, but then Danny proposed to you, so I never said anything. My master might get upset with me for saying this, but we were talking about you before you got engaged."

Kitten froze, the wine bottle halfway to her lips. She carefully put the bottle down on the windowsill and stared at Marie.

"You really are," Kitten blurted. "You really want me to join your house!"

Marie was confused by both the non sequitur and the blooming embarrassment coloring Kitten's cheeks. The girl met Marie's gaze and then looked away, tears welling up. The older slave stood up, crossed the room, and embraced the younger girl.

"Kitten, sweetie, you know how fond I am of you. And Quentin thinks highly of you; so do Gary and Jack, for that matter. That's not...we weren't discussing you in that way. Quentin has his hands full with us three."

Marie simply held Kitten for a minute before pulling back from the embrace, her hands still on the girl's shoulders. The girl's face was a map of confusion and dashed hope, and Marie made a snap decision. "Kitten, what I'm about to say doesn't leave this conversation, do you understand?"

"Yes, ma'am," Kitten replied.

"You said that it seemed like I was on a different level. That's because I am. So are Jack and Gary. Kitten, what if I were to tell you that Master purchased me off the auction block? That I'd never laid eyes on him before he bought me? That I had another owner before him?"

"How?"

"I won't go into details right now. I can't. Kitten, I chose to enter slavery of my own free will. It's where I belong. If you truly desire to be owned, at a level far more intense than the soft world you see out that window..." Marie gestured at the leather-clad masses below. "The possibility exists for you to do that. You can be the slave you need to be."

Kitten's eyes were filled with stars and wonder. "How does it all work?"

"I've said too much already. We'll talk about it sometime in the next few days, I promise. I want you to swear that you won't discuss it with anyone, okay?" Marie could see the questions dancing behind Kitten's eyes, but Kitten just nodded.

"I promise. But it better be soon!"

"I'll try," Marie said. "I really have to go take back over for Gary or Master will have my ass." She kissed Kitten on the cheek. "Love you, girl!" She rushed out the door without waiting for a reply.

She didn't get the opportunity to tell Quentin about her talk with Kitten until breakfast the next morning. He was furious, and although he had to leave after breakfast for an all-day meeting, he left little doubt that there would be repercussions when he arrived home. He texted Marie in the afternoon with her instructions for when he arrived home.

Marie knelt in front of Quentin's favorite armchair, her outward serenity hiding the turmoil in her mind, when Quentin walked through the front door. His two golden retrievers ran to meet him but didn't bark, their training every bit as meticulous as that of his slaves. He disappeared into the kitchen without acknowledging her.

She knew Quentin's routine; Gary was in the kitchen, pouring him a snifter of Scotch, kneeling, and presenting it to him. That was normally her duty when he arrived home. She felt a pang of regret as she waited for Quentin; she took pleasure in helping him relax after work each day with that small act of service.

He walked back into the room a minute later, sat down, and sipped his drink.

"You told me what happened this morning, and although I had to leave before we could finish, I want to know why. Enlighten me." His voice was tightly controlled.

Marie kept her gaze aimed at his feet and spoke softly. "Sir, I beg that you will allow me to apologize. I should not have taken it upon myself to speak to Kitten about matters relating, even tangentially, to the Marketplace without your permission. I overstepped my bounds and have no excuse for my actions."

"Apology noted," Quentin said. "Continue."

"Sir, we had planned to spot Kitten and offer her the opportunity to join the Marketplace several months ago," Marie said. "This was interrupted by her engagement. I had hoped things would work out for their sake, but I didn't expect it to, and last night's conversation confirmed that. If Kitten gets married to Danny, it won't last. She fell for him because he was the first guy to give her something approximating what she's looking for. She's frustrated but doesn't know how to find something better.

"She is, in my professional opinion, an ideal candidate. She's got incredibly strong service instincts. She's intelligent. She's conscientious, and she has a deep-seated need to belong somewhere, which manifests itself in a desire for structure and ownership. She's in good physical condition. She's attractive, and her youthful appearance could be a plus in some markets. She presents as the goth/riot grrl from hell but Sir, before I was spotted, I was wearing gang colors. She needs what the Marketplace can offer her."

"You made your case four months ago, slave. I agreed with you, but when she became engaged, the parameters shifted. Instead of inviting her to join our house and evaluating her before gradually revealing the Marketplace like we would with any other client, we'd have to reveal the Marketplace to her first. I concur that she would probably accept the offer, but we've lost a measure of control over the situation by not having her here and acclimated before discussing the Marketplace. How dare you drop hints to her without clearing it with me?"

Marie closed her eyes for a second as Quentin's words sunk in. She had failed to consider the ramifications of her actions. She wanted to apologize again, but kept her mouth shut; he took a breath to continue, and she couldn't interrupt him. It would only make things worse.

"Also, if she were to break off her engagement to Danny and immediately come to stay with us, there would be the impression that our household had...lured her away from her fiancé. It could become very public and damage our standing in the Atlanta kink community. Danny would go ballistic if she left him and immediately came here, and it would be very difficult to hide that she's here given how active we are now. This community is our primary source of potential clients; burning that bridge would have consequences for us that may not be worth one client."

Possible responses sparked through her mind, live wires that she was afraid to touch, but she couldn't let her silence cost Kitten the chance to enter the Marketplace. She spoke quickly, before fear of the consequences could change her mind. "We could cross that bridge when we get to it, Sir, just like we have with every other slave who's had to break personal ties when entering the Marketplace. It could be spun as us giving her a place to stay until she moves away..."

His hand moved like a striking cobra, backhanding her so viciously that her head snapped to the side. Her cheek burned from the fiery imprint of his fingers, but she bit her lip and returned her gaze to his shoes.

"That's not your call," Quentin said. Fury crackled in his voice. "I've been spotting for ten years. Yes, you assist me, but I am the one who certifies the quality of our clients to the trainers we work with, and I am the one responsible to the Marketplace for safeguarding its secrecy."

He got up and paced. "You are my slave. The burden of

responsibility is on me. One misjudged potential client could lead to the Marketplace going viral on Kinkynet or elsewhere on the internet. The Marketplace has always had enough connections to keep people from getting taken too seriously on the talk-show circuit, but social media is a thousand times more dangerous. Can you imagine the damage a Sharon Brosa could do in this era?"

Marie had never felt so much shame. She had not considered the potential ramifications when she told Kitten about her true status; she had been so convinced of Kitten's need and suitability for the Marketplace that she had truly overstepped her boundaries. She had failed her owner and the trust he had placed in her. There was only one way she could think of to show her shame and remorse. She bent forward slowly, stretching her arms in front of her, prostrating herself before her owner.

"You allowed your personal feelings about Kitten to interfere with your professional duties," Quentin said. "I decided to hold off on spotting her when she became engaged. If you thought we should revisit the decision, you should have come to me first. I've trusted you to identify candidates, to evaluate them and share those evaluations with me even when I disagree, and to manage and teach them once we bring them in for pre-training. I trusted you in every stage of the process to act as my surrogate. You do not, however, make decisions."

A bell sounded softly in the dining room, signaling that Gary was ready to serve dinner. Quentin stood up without another word and walked away, leaving Marie alone with her thoughts; she stayed absolutely still.

She had been so proud when Quentin sent her to Ken Mandarin for training as a spotter, in order that she might assist him. She'd been proud to take so much of the burden off of her owner's shoulders, and even prouder as the months and years passed and Quentin allowed her to take more responsibility. It had been her idea to start hosting the monthly play party, and Quentin had rewarded her brainstorm by taking her to the Academy with him, not only as his personal attendant, but to help present their paper on spotting techniques in the age of Kinkynet.

She'd let him down and betrayed his trust. She had signed a fresh six-year contract with him two years ago, a contract that recognized her training as a spotter instead of a general purpose slave and included a clause that if she chose to leave service after satisfactorily completing her contract, Quentin would sponsor her to become a spotter in her own right. She'd never been so proud as she was when she signed it.

Now she had ruined everything. She could still hear the voice of her trainer, Sebastian Pettibone Tucker, in her mind. "Pride is a double-edged sword. You must be driven by pride in a job well done, but it must be a quiet pride. Your pride should show only in the results of your work, the satisfactory completion of your orders, and the drive to obey and improve yourself. Take pride in performing any role you're assigned well, but do not allow yourself to become proud of the role itself; it leads to dissension and blunts the edge of your service to your owner."

She had taken too much pride in her role. She had discovered a gift for spotting; she was able to channel her innate desire to help people, the drive for service that had gotten her spotted years before, into the desire to find others like her and help them find their place in the Marketplace. She knew that at the end of her contract, she would probably leave service and become a spotter on her own. Would Quentin take away her role as his spotting assistant? She couldn't deny that she deserved to have that taken away, but would she still have a place in his household at all?

Marie knew Kitten belonged in the Marketplace. That was a professional estimation, not an emotional one. The emotional decision had been revealing the Marketplace to Kitten. She wanted to crawl to Quentin and beg her forgiveness, but absolution would only come—if it came at all—on his time.

She heard him go upstairs, heard Jack and Gary eating their dinner in the kitchen after Gary cleared the plates from the dining room. It was almost an hour before she felt a touch on her shoulder; she rose back to a kneeling position and Gary hooked a leash onto her collar. When he tugged the leash upward, she stumbled as she rose, her knees stiff from holding her position for so long. She regained her balance and he led her out to the dungeon.

"I fucked up so bad," Marie whispered as Gary closed the dungeon door behind them. A single tear traced down her cheekbone, but she fought the torrent that tried to follow it, knowing that Quentin could walk in at any moment.

Gary glanced at the door, then leaned forward and silently kissed the tear away. He led her across the room, fastened cuffs around her wrists, and snapped them into place with her facing the cross. He held up a big leather gag and she opened her mouth, silently giving thanks. She knew that the gag was an object of mercy.

When Gary was finished, he stepped to the side. Out of the corner of her eye, she watched him assume a position of attention next to the cross. She closed her eyes and thought of how many times she'd been in this exact same position, her skin tingling with anticipation as she prepared to take pain for Quentin's pleasure. Knowing that she was bound here for discipline only brought her more shame.

She heard the door open. She heard Quentin walk in and dismiss Gary, and it took a conscious effort of will not to turn her head, not to try and communicate through her eyes how sorry she was.

Then she felt his touch. His fingers wrapped around the back of her neck. His grip triggered her tears; her bonds gave them the freedom to fall. She gave in to her tears, and they fell like petals from a rose, each one an offering of contrition. His touch reassured her. She knew that Quentin wouldn't discipline her if he planned to release her from service.

She felt him step away. Her back was straight and her head held high, though she could no longer see the wall through her tears. She heard the squeak of Quentin's whip cabinet opening and reminded herself to oil it the next morning, despite her fear and shame.

A cracking sound telegraphed the first touch of the whip, and all she knew was fire.

The first snap of the whip carved a line of flame across her skin. She bit down on the gag to keep from screaming. The second strike crossed the first, a back-burn of agony, and her whole world became nothing but pain and reaction.

The gag muffled Marie's screams, but her tears continued to flow. Each crack brought another explosion of fire across her skin, penetrating through to her core. She went limp, hanging from her bonds. She struggled to straighten up. The whip crashed across her back and she collapsed again. The whip never gave her a chance to gather herself; her world was nothing but the rhythm of fire, the flame of impact, and, once she lost the strength to scream, her wracked sobbing.

She had no idea how long it lasted. It could have been days. Her whole world was sorrow and shame, redemption through pain. She thought she felt blood running down her back, but he didn't stop. It all started to blend together until she could no longer discern individual strikes. She had never been hurt like this, even on those nights in training when Tucker was testing her pain tolerance. Her conscious thoughts faded to nothing but the strikes that carved through her skin and her soul.

❧

Marie hung limply from her bonds, gasping around the gag for air. Quentin touched the back of her neck and rotated her head to face him. She began to weep quietly as she realized the whipping had ended.

His hand grasped her chin. She tried to stand, but every muscle in her body was a live wire, sparking and melting. She leaned toward him, trying to kiss his hand, but the leather panel of the gag wouldn't let her. She settled for closing her eyes and leaning into it, the touch of her owner providing her comfort.

Quentin pulled his hand away after a few seconds. She moved

her head in the direction his hand had gone, still trying to nuzzle it, only to freeze when she felt his grip on the back of her neck again. He pressed her forward into the cross, holding her with one hand, and then unsnapped each cuff.

She didn't know if she could stand when he let go. Every muscle in her body was a light bulb flickering, dying slowly. "Down," he said, and she hesitated before the gentle pressure of his fingers guided her slowly onto her knees.

She felt him let go and stayed where he had left her until she heard him speak. "Come," he said. She turned around on her knees to face him, every movement a symphony of razorblades. He was seated ten feet away in a leather-wrapped chair, facing her.

She began to crawl. Stiffly, a few inches at a time, she traversed the impossible distance to her owner, his boots her only landmark.

She knelt in front of him, eyes downcast. "Get back on all fours and stay there. Over here," he said, pointing, and she shifted into the position he had indicated. He lifted his boots and lowered them onto her back.

The muted embers of her wounds reignited at the weight of his legs resting on her back; she bit down into the gag to keep from crying out. She remained still even as his heels dug into the wounds left by the whip.

Quentin had used her for a footstool before; she remembered the feeling of contentment at being useful, remembered clearing her mind of all but her place under his feet. She couldn't find that place now; the weight on her wounds kept her grounded in the moment.

As the minutes passed, though, her mind slid into that contented head space. The pain that had been reawakened faded and, aside from one small part of her mind that awaited instructions, she let her mind drift free. She thought about the years she'd spent as a slave, the contentment she'd found in knowing her place, the simple beauty she'd found in service. She'd come so far, from the crime-ridden projects of New Orleans to this beautiful house on a hill. The Marketplace had given her everything she had become.

All she had ever wanted was to be useful.

This is my place, she thought to herself, and she simply waited for her owner's next command.

"Kneel up," Quentin said and swung his legs off of her back. She responded with the instincts that years of training and service had granted her. Her physical movements were slowed by the pain that still rippled through her body, but her attention snapped back instantly at the sound of her owner's voice. He waited patiently for her to finish kneeling.

When she was upright, he wrapped his right hand around the top of her head. He pulled her down, her face rubbing the inseam of his jeans.

She didn't know what he wanted her to do; the thick leather panel of the gag was still in her way. She nuzzled his inner thighs, rubbing against him. From this angle, she couldn't see his face, but his hand was still on her head and kept pressing her forward. Her whole attention was on the thin layer of denim between her gag and his cock. She rubbed up and down despite the obstacle.

His other hand reached behind her head and unbuckled the gag; it fell to the floor under them, covered in her drool. She worked her jaw for a second before his hand guided her back down. She sought out the bulge in his jeans with her lips and tongue, trying to please him through her confusion. Quentin had never before used her sexually when punishing her.

She heard foil tear; he dropped a condom onto his thigh and then unzipped his pants. A slashing pain radiated from her shoulder to the middle of her back as she dipped her neck to grasp the condom in her mouth. She suppressed the pain and lowered her head again, unrolling it along his cock in one smooth motion.

Quentin's hand tightened, holding her head still. "I want you to masturbate for me," he said and pulled his hand away. She pulled as he released her, taking a breath. She ignored the pain of her muscles and slid her lips back down his shaft again, taking him in as deeply as she could. Her hand delved between her legs, one finger seeking out her clit and rolling over it in a circular motion. Part of her mind was surprised at how wet she was despite the pain that echoed through her body; it only took seconds for her arousal to bury any attempt to think about what was happening.

More bolts of pain shot across her body as she bobbed her head up and down. She flicked her tongue around and across his cock, worshiping it, and then took it all the way in again. A muffled sound emanated from her throat as her body responded to the crossing waves of pleasure and pain.

Her lips slid up and down his cock faster as she became more aroused, trying instinctively to make him orgasm as she edged closer to her own. She wanted to look at him, to beg permission for her orgasm with her eyes, but she didn't dare, and then he pulled his cock free of her mouth. "Stop."

She pulled her finger away and returned to her kneeling position, hands resting on her thighs, awaiting a command. Her arousal faded away slowly, her breathing becoming more regular. Quentin zipped his pants back up.

"Look at me," he said, and she followed his instructions, meeting his gaze for the first time since he'd arrived home. "Your role is to serve me. Whether as a spotter or a footstool, with your mind or body, you are here to serve."

He waited a minute before continuing. "You may," he said simply.

She began to cry again as she knelt down. As she kissed each boot, she could taste the salt of her tears mixing with the earthy scent of leather. Her lips brushed across his boot, covering every inch of them she could reach.

Each ache was a reminder of redemption, each kiss a demonstration of gratitude. She could have stayed on her hands and knees forever, showing Quentin with each touch of her lips how much she needed her place at his feet. He waited patiently as she made her atonement, far beyond the ritualistic single kiss he expected on the toe of each boot.

Quentin finally cleared his throat, and she returned to her

kneeling position. "Thank you, Sir, for your guidance and correction. I will endeavor to do better in the future," Marie said in the formula that Quentin expected.

"Your apology from earlier is accepted," Quentin said. "I've spoken to both Mandarin and Tucker. They agree that you should get a second chance. I will be placing a report about the incident in your file and reporting the incident to the Marketplace as a precaution. Other than that, we'll consider the matter behind us."

"Thank you, Sir," Marie said. "Thank you. I didn't realize the magnitude of my actions until you explained them to me. I am deeply ashamed of my...hubris. I took too much pride in my role and I overstepped my bounds. Sir, my pride should solely reside in being allowed to serve you and your house."

Quentin nodded. "I've reviewed Kitten's file," he said after a moment. "Tomorrow, you will contact her and arrange a meeting. I would like you to prepare for that meeting and think about how to handle the logistical issues should she accept our offer now or in the future."

"Yes, Sir. Thank you, Sir." Marie said, stifling her surprise. She thought she'd blown Kitten's chance.

Quentin crossed the room and pressed a button on the intercom; a minute later, Gary walked back into the dungeon.

"Clean her wounds and put her in the cage for the night," Quentin said. Marie hated the cage, but all she could think about was that she was allowed to stay.

"May I, Sir?" she asked. Quentin walked over and stood in front of her. She kissed the toe of his boot again. "Thank you, Sir, for being lenient with this slave."

"Don't make me regret it." Quentin walked out of the room.

Marie put her fork down a second after Quentin did; when her owner was finished with dinner, so was she. Kitten glanced between them and hurriedly put her fork down as well.

Jack walked into the dining room seconds later and picked up Quentin's plate. Kitten stood to assist him in clearing the table.

"Sit down," Quentin said. "You'll have plenty of time to serve if you join the Marketplace. Right now, you're a guest."

Kitten sat, blushing. "Yes, sir." Marie smiled at the girl as Jack deftly gathered the dinner plates.

"Apple pie, Sir?" Jack asked.

"In a little while. With plenty of ice cream for each of us," Quentin said, smiling at Kitten and Marie. Jack nodded and left the room.

"May I go smoke?" Kitten asked. "I've still got a billion questions floating in my head, but I need a minute."

"You'll definitely have to give that up if you go into training," Quentin said with a mock-reproving tone. "Go for it. You're not in training yet."

Kitten giggled, rose, and retrieved her cigarettes from her purse. She slipped out the door.

"Give her a few minutes and then follow her."

Marie nodded. Quentin walked out of the room and Marie carried the rest of the dinnerware into the kitchen, and then slipped out the door.

❧

"Do you need some time to yourself or may I join you?" Marie asked, walking up behind Kitten. The girl was seated on the low stone wall surrounding the terrace, looking up at the stars.

"Of course you can."

Marie sat down next to her. "I used to be in a gang, you know."

"Really?"

"Back in New Orleans. I grew up in a project, thought the gang was my only way out. I got busted. Probation and community service. I ended up doing it at the Humane Society, and the volunteer coordinator there took me under her wing. She got me off the streets, moved me into her house, and made me study for my GED. She told me she'd help me get a job. A few weeks after I moved in, she came home and found me naked in her bed, wanting to thank her with the only currency I had."

Marie looked at Kitten and remembered what it was like to be twenty-two and have no idea where she belonged in the world.

"We talked for hours that night, and she took me in hand. Months later, she told me about the Marketplace. She saved my life. I needed to belong to something bigger than myself. Maybe if I hadn't found the Marketplace, I would have ended up joining the army or something, but I probably would have ended up back in the gang.

"I have to emphasize to you, that this life is not about kinky sex. It's about service. I'd never been into kinky sex before I was spotted. I was just another L9 girl. Miss Devereaux, my spotter, saw in me the need to devote myself to something greater than myself, the need for structure and control. I see that in you.

"The Marketplace carefully vets owners. You'll be safe. But you may have an owner who's not physically attractive to you or one that is not buying you to be sexually available. You can't look at this house and expect it all to be like this."

"But you've been happy?" Kitten put out her cigarette and lit another one.

"Yes, I have. You told me once that you grew up in a trailer park. Sweetie, I grew up in the worst projects in New Orleans. I was too poor to ever have a choice about anything. This is a choice.

"You make a choice when you sign your contract. You get what you need, but you make the choice and you live with it. If you run, if you break that contract, you'll never get another chance, and I think for you that would be a tragedy. This is where you belong, Kitten. I want you to be sure this is what you want, though. It's the biggest decision you've ever made."

"I just... Danny's a good man. He loves me. A part of me wants to keep trying to make it work. At the same time, all I've been able to think about since the party is being owned. A part of me wants to start right now, a part of me is terrified, and the rest of me is somewhere in between." Kitten paused. "You know how much I look up to you. This is a lot to think about, though. I'm... overwhelmed."

"You don't have to make your mind up tonight. The last thing Mr. Yardley or I want to do is pressure you. I'll drive you home whenever you're ready to leave, and the invitation is out there when you're ready."

"I don't think I want to ever leave," Kitten said. They sat in companionable silence for a while; Marie watched Kitten look at the stars. She seemed lost in them, and Marie quietly stood, intending to leave the girl alone to think. The Marketplace had saved her life, but it had still taken time for her to be ready to take the plunge. She knew Kitten would be no different.

Before Marie could walk away, Kitten rose and wrapped her in an embrace. They stood there for several minutes, arms around each other, Kitten's head tucked into Marie's shoulder. Kitten finally stepped back. "Thank you," she said quietly.

"I know you'll make the decision that's best for you. And I'll always be here for you either way." Marie smiled, turned, and walked back toward the welcoming lights of home.

Kitten sat down on the wall again, looking out at the stars, thinking of the beat-up trailer she left behind, the endless chain of boyfriends her mother brought home, the night she turned sixteen and walked away from the trailer park forever. "Somewhere to belong," she whispered to herself. She located Orion with the practiced eyes of a lifelong stargazer, and smiled as she envisioned his belt as a collar.

Foreword

I was fortunate enough to find myself reading multiple stories by the same authors and having the luxurious and painful editorial task of choosing just one story from each. But there are always exceptions. In addition to the speech opening this collection, this writer gave me the only story concerning someone who was once in the Marketplace but then walked away by choice, leaving behind baffled friends and fellow professionals for a world much less concerned with formal roles. And yet, our real world has its own expectations, fantasies and social structures demanding rituals and customary gestures and grand schemes. Which is how people who can easily wend their way through the Byzantine layers of protocol and deference in a secretive slave-trading world can be completely flummoxed by something as ordinary as a proposal of marriage. Especially when, despite leaving the Marketplace as a participant, the urges and desires that drove you to be there still remain in your heart.

I also like that this tale is connected to the other one by the same author. As someone who loves revisiting my own world and characters, I like weaving and expanding worlds in a storyteller's mind.

Marie Casey Stevens is still the same person she was when she wrote A Thousand Things Before Breakfast, the piece opening this collection. More or less.

Coals for the New Castle
Marie Casey Stevens

The mid-morning breeze wafted gentle into Charlotte's sunny kitchen. The room reflected the woman's calm warmth and preference for detail and order perfectly. Subtle yellow walls caught the light, a small radio turned to a local classical station improved the atmosphere without intruding upon it, and an impeccable coffee service sat invitingly on the table. Only two details of the scene stood in sharp contrast to an otherwise perfect demonstration of successful hospitality.

Upon Charlotte's face, many times compared to Anne Bancroft's over the years, trembling lips fought to keep a persistent crooked smile from splitting to let laughter escape.

And across from her at the table, a man in his mid-thirties radiated confusion, dismay, and sincere bewilderment in stark opposition to his surroundings. Even his short inky black hair seemed to emit a distress call, lurching upward and outward in every direction obviously traumatized by repeated agitated finger-combing. Julian's foot tapped erratically on the mosaic tiled floor, and the long fingers of his left hand sketched a formless pattern on the table. His right hand followed up yet another eye roll of despair by passing over his face, and Charlotte's shoulders visibly quivered with restrained laughter as the man erupted again.

"It's not even like that cliché about what you get for the woman who has everything! You know her!"

Fighting not to chuckle at his despair, Charlotte nodded. "Beyond books and coffee, Magda does have a terminal case of acquisition apathy." She put her coffee down, the sound of the empty ceramic touching the saucer prompting immediate action. Arnold, her house slave of twelve years, entered the room. Unobtrusively, he poured her a fresh coffee and added both sugar and a touch of cream. The two exchanged the briefest of looks, and the tall man's eyes crinkled with discreet mirth. Then, face smoothed, he placed a fresh bottle of water in front of Julian.

"Thank you," the younger man said, calming a fraction at etiquette's demand.

Arnold nodded, his sandy close-cropped hair flashing in the sunlight, and exited as quietly as he'd appeared.

Charlotte sipped her coffee and observed in a carefully casual tone, "You seem to think she might not accept."

Julian convulsed, inhaling his water in a combined gasp and snort. He shook his head, eyes watering. "Yes, Charlotte, I think she might turn me down. She might just think knowing me for twenty years hasn't exactly proven that marrying me and putting up with me for another twenty or forty more is the best offer she can get. Didn't you tell her something like that once? Or twice? Or a few dozen times?"

"Different times, and you were different people," Charlotte said serenely.

"Some things haven't changed," he shot back. "She still hates diamonds. And she's color-blind! How the hell do you pick stones for that?" The picture of dejection, he crumpled and put his head in his hands. "I'm just terrible at this."

"Yes. You suck at it." Charlotte permitted an open snicker as Julian's head snapped up. "You have no talent for conventional marriage proposals. Look on the bright side. Maybe you'll have no talent for creating a conventional divorce. You've almost got it right, though."

"Do tell," Julian challenged, but her merry eyes ignored the sarcasm.

"What do you do for the woman who has everything she thinks she wants?" Her black eyebrows arched towards her iron-gray hair. "You've done some wonderful things for her. Propose that way. Give her something she wants you to do."

The words sliced through the sharp edges of his anxiety, smoothing his fractured panic to focus. "Something she wants me to do…"

"She must have mentioned something," Charlotte drawled, heaping helpings of innuendo on each vowel. "The Magda I know has few problems being vocal."

"She did, just the other day. After you had us over for that lovely dinner." Julian nodded slowly. "I can't figure out the logistics of it, though."

"Why don't you tell me, and we'll see what we can put together?"

Five minutes later, Charlotte called for Arnold and issued instructions. He left for a moment, returned with a pencil and a sketchpad and sat at her feet. Silently he worked while Julian and his owner continued to discuss the matter. The slave only spoke three times: once to provide the name of a business, once to provide an estimate of time to allot for its services, and once to answer a question from Julian after receiving his owner's permission to speak freely.

"I would be profoundly honored, sir," Arnold began. "She trained me, and I would be grateful for the opportunity to be of service for such a momentous occasion as this."

Something about the older man's absolute sincerity and dignity resonated with Julian, replacing the last vestiges of nervousness with a peaceful determination. Using his phone, he took down the list of items Charlotte and Arnold said he would need until Charlotte arrived at the last one. Raising his eyebrows, he reached into the inner pocket of his leather jacket and extricated a velvet box. With a hint of defiance, he placed it on the table and slid it gently towards the woman.

"If you have a problem with this, Charlotte, now's the time to speak up."

"You were different people at a different time," she repeated, and tapped the box lightly with a fingernail. "How long have you had this?"

"Two months, nine days."

With the grin of a child allowed to share in an adult conspiracy, Charlotte reached for the box and opened it. "Oh, my..."

"Well?"

"These couldn't be more perfect, Julian." She examined the contents for a few more seconds and snapped the lid shut as her eyes began to water. "Simply perfect. Now, Arnold will take you to Rorschach's Test. After you're done, you'll get her gift certificate and pick up the items on your list. Leave the certificate there. I'll bring Magda there when she's done with work. You and Arnold will go to your apartment to have everything ready by the time I bring her home. Have I missed anything, or is that the plan?"

Julian glanced down at his forearms, his right hand touching the space below his outer wrist that a watch face would cover if he wore one. He looked at Arnold's sketchpad and nodded, bringing a bright smile to the slave's face. "That is indeed the plan."

Two and a half hours later at five o'clock, as Julian and Arnold chatted in the car en route to Julian and Magda's apartment, Charlotte drove to fetch her friend from work.

⁂

Outside a grey office building, the young woman sat cross-legged and unmoving on the sidewalk. The charcoal tank top, cardigan, and matching ankle-length skirt might have made her a nondescript and camouflaged part of the scenery, just another woman in her late thirties of short stature waiting for her ride, save for three things.

First, she didn't look up repeatedly, searching for whomever she expected to arrive for her. Her stillness set her apart; in a sea of people impatient to get home, Magda read with such patience the air around her seemed to move less. Even other people standing nearby, exhausted and waiting for the bus, showed more signs of animation.

Second, her shock of chin-length vivid red curls vibrated with every breath of breeze, the startling Irish red a merry affront to the starkly grey professional attire. That, combined with the lack of affected dignity inherent in her comfortable seat on the sidewalk gave passers by an impression of a woman roughly a decade or more younger than Magda's thirty-seven years.

Third, upon hearing Charlotte's vintage Volvo and rising, Magda removed her cardigan to reveal intricate tattoos that swirled from her inner forearms around to her biceps and up to her shoulders. With a wide smile she ran to the car, hair and tattoos flashing in the sun. Heads turned to watch her flurry of unaffected delight upon seeing her friend, smiles appearing on work-weary visages in her wake.

"Where's Julian? This is a surprise!" Magda slid into the passenger's seat and frowned. "Is everything okay?"

"Yes, Mugwump," Charlotte said fondly. "Don't get started worrying." Grinning, Charlotte pulled into traffic. "Julian and I talked a little longer than we planned, and when he mentioned picking you up I seized the chance to spend some time with my best friend. Problem with that?" She arched her eyebrows in mock challenge.

"Of course not! How did your coffee with him go?"

"Besides the fact that the unnatural man doesn't drink coffee?" She rolled her eyes. "It went fine, sweetie. You can stop fretting that I'm going to take his head off."

"I wasn't," Magda protested faintly.

"You nearly made panic your very own butt plug, Mugwump. And yes, once he may have deserved anything we who cared about you could have thrown at him. You gave him more than a few bruises of the wrong kind, too. Complicated history you two have managed to acquire."

"We've known each other for twenty years, though. That tends to accrue a history."

"People go their whole lives without racking up one like yours. You've both changed, though… and I have an idea of how he feels about you. How do you feel these days?"

"Good! Thanks for the advice about that temp agency. You were right. I actually have the time to look around and see what's out there." She laughed. "Some of these places need remedial English more than they need an interpreter."

"That doesn't surprise me. I can see you've finally gotten some sleep, too. By the way, that's for you." Charlotte gestured at a fast food bag in the center console next to a soda and a bottle of water.

"Dinner? Where are we going?"

"It's a surprise, and we have a forty-five minute drive. Dig in, kiddo, and let's talk. There's a crinkle in your crinolines—I can see it on your face. Spill it."

Magda pulled a French fry out of the bag, shoulders slumping. "It's nothing. Half ordinary, half embarrassing, all pathetic. Let's skip it."

"What's that phrase you use?" Charlotte tapped her teeth with a fingernail in mock concentration. "Oh, yes? Fuck that noise. Look at all the ordinary, embarrassing pathetic you've got on me. Remember the duct tape complexion strip incident?"

"I said those things worked like duct tape! I didn't say they were duct tape!" Magda's white cheeks flushed with a pink blush that clashed jarringly with her freckles.

"I still don't own duct tape to this day. Come on. Start with the ordinary, but start spilling it."

"They're kind of mixed together." Magda took a deep breath and squared her shoulders. "Okay. Julian offered to play soft slave and I froze." She paused, shaking her head.

"Oh, sweetie! That happens, and you know it! Sometimes you're just not game for it!"

"I was! But I haven't trained since..." her voice trailed off, twelve years encapsulated in that pause. Mercifully, her friend finished the thought for her.

"Since you trained Arnold, fell in love with a man with conventional preferences and spent some years happy with him until things changed. Mugwump, when you left—"

"I know," Magda began to interrupt, but her friend didn't relinquish the conversation at her exasperation. Instead, she continued in a firmer voice.

"No, we're talking about this now," Charlotte insisted quietly…but implacably. "When you left the Marketplace for a conventional relationship nearly a thousand miles from everyone you knew, you baffled all of us. You had such potential! One of the youngest senior trainers we'd ever seen, clearly dedicated and seemingly happy one day. Virtually the next day, you'd packed up every part of this life and headed off for one that had none of this in it. Maybe we should have expected it, but you left your collar behind, and all of your training. Were you ever happy with the Marketplace?"

"Of course!" Startled, Magda stared at her friend. "Of course I was! It was my life!"

"Then why did you leave it? Not just for something different, sweetie, but for something that was as close to the exact opposite as you could get this far north of the Bible Belt? For something that none of us thought was you!" Charlotte's exasperation rocked Magda's chin back; her words conveyed near-personal affront as much as bewilderment.

"I'm not just what you thought I was!" For the first time in their friendship, anger colored Magda's cheeks in response to her friend's words. "I'm not just a trainer, and I'm not just a slave. I'm a person, and I met a person who made me happy for who he was. He may have brought something different to the table, but I loved it just as much."

"Is that what you were looking for?" Charlotte asked gently.

"He was. Who he was. William, not whether William liked floggers or was a top or a bottom or Marketplace or not. I'm sorry to be so complicated, Charlotte, but it's not 'this or that' here. I wasn't looking for Marketplace or soft world or vanilla or fucking Rocky Road. I was looking for the person, and I found him. He happened to not be in the Marketplace, that happened to not be his thing, and I left to be with him."

"Did you miss it?"

"Of course. I also missed the weather back home, and the smell of the wind off the lake, and my favorite newspaper."

Charlotte nodded. "Fair enough. Did you ever regret it?"

"No. I was happy—we were happy—until we weren't any more. And I wouldn't trade that time for anything."

Charlotte paused, considering. She'd known the end of the story, but until this moment hadn't pushed to learn the beginning of it. "Have you even ever had a Marketplace boyfriend?"

"No, I haven't," Magda said softly.

Charlotte spared her a brief but searching glance as she drove. "Why not?"

"It just turned out that way. I don't date trainees or former trainees, a collared trainer isn't an owner's girlfriend, and my peers were all in collared service. The people who wanted long-term relationships always came from the outside world, and things just got compartmentalized."

"And Julian has now asked you to mix them together," Charlotte said in the tone of one supplying a newly discovered answer to a math problem.

"Exactly. My head went into contradiction overload. I wanted to take that control so much, but I didn't want to lose the feeling that we're equals. Even though that makes for some power struggles sometimes... I like it."

"You think you'd break him?" Charlotte's eyebrows went up to full mast.

"Probably not, but would I see him the same way again? Would he see me the same way again? I don't know." Magda sighed. "We've already gone through so much..."

"You don't want to risk anything." Charlotte nodded to herself. "Understandable. Wrong answer, but understandable. You don't want to risk changing him. You don't want to risk him running away in disgust when you show him a different part of yourself."

Magda's ears turned pink and she bowed her head. "Yes. We've joked about it over the years, but it would hurt so much if I showed him that part and he hated it."

"That's not the problem," Charlotte muttered, taking an exit off the interstate.

"What?" Magda asked, pulling a burger from the bag.

"Have there been other problems?" Charlotte asked, blinking widely at Magda.

Magda's head dropped, but not before Charlotte saw ruddy color subsume Magda's face in a blush so fierce it looked painful. "Yes."

"Oh, sweetie, it's okay." She spared a hand from the steering wheel to quickly smooth the younger woman's riotous hair. "What happened?"

"We were just throwing words back and forth, goofing around, and for a split second I slipped."

Charlotte's face smoothed in worry, imagining truly terrible scenarios. "What did you do?"

"I almost tried to bring him to formal manners," Magda admitted. "It shocked the hell out of him, and me, too."

I'll bet, thought Charlotte. "I've got an idea, Mugwump. You love concrete proof. So when Julian does something you've said you want him to do, accept the evidence as it builds up. Then," Charlotte said firmly, "when he offers up control, believe he really wants you to take it."

"And if I screw it up?" Magda looked up, green eyes wide with thirst for any answer but her own projected worst-case scenarios.

"Then take a breath and remind yourself even perfectionists are never perfect! You made one mistake, and the pair of you will make more. If you were talking about anyone else, you'd know that—and say it. Tell me he's never a pulled a...what do you call it..." Charlotte drummed her nails on the steering wheel fiercely and then slapped it victoriously. "An epic fail! That's it! Tell me he's never pulled an epic fail of any kind in bed with you before."

Magda choked on her soda, and Charlotte nodded smugly. "No need to tell me what it was." She considered. "Well, maybe later. But he didn't truly fail, did he? You didn't ban him from the premises, so to speak. I know you take training seriously, but you weren't training Julian then—and you're not now. He's asking you to play together, Mugwump! He's not asking you to train him. Regardless of what you two have been though, you have to quit walking on eggshells eventually."

"But—" Magda protested.

"Yes, yes. We must care for what we care about. Let's say you'll have to just stomp on some of those eggshells—some of them—until they don't make noise anymore. Or just call it quits now." Charlotte paused, considering her words, and continued. "You entered the Marketplace with the Kasden legacy looming over you, determined to live up to Aunt Jorgean and you did. There weren't many senior slaves younger than you when you were one, and almost no junior trainers younger than you when you reached that point. You always lacked one thing, though, and few of us wanted to say it."

Magda looked up from her hands quickly, concerned at a perceived failure. "What?"

"You never had the balanced life. You lived in the Marketplace like an academic who never leaves the campus. Your friends worried you were missing out on a part of life, and some in the Marketplace worried about its effect on your training. How could you truly understand and train people who had all the life experiences you were missing?"

Magda's eyes lost their focus, only appearing to look through the windshield as she chewed on her friend's assessment. "Maybe you're right."

"Speaking of stopping now, we've reached our destination!" Charlotte neatly parallel parked the Volvo and turned off the engine.

"Rorschach's Test?" Magda squealed. "You're getting ink? I don't believe it! You're getting ink, and I get to be there?"

"Stranger things have happened," Charlotte answered blithely. "Could you bring that bottle of water? You told me once a person getting a tattoo should have some."

"Yes, I did!" Red curls vibrating with glee, Magda scooped up the bottle and hurried to open the door. Charlotte walked through it with a nod and strode across the gleaming blonde wood floor to the counter. It stood in the middle of a large waiting room, an open and bright airy space surrounded by thousands of pieces of tattoo flash art. Before she could speak, however, Magda rushed behind the counter to hug the proprietor.

"Holbein! It's been too long!"

At well over six feet, the tanned bald man had to bend at the waist and knees to return the hug, picking up the short woman easily. In opposition to Magda's ebullience, he moved with the caution-learned slowness big men acquire in deference to those around them. Only his light blue eyes moved quickly, noting all the details of every person who entered his establishment. "You're not kidding, Miss Underfoot," he replied in a low rumble, planting a kiss on top of her head as he set her down.

"Miss Underfoot?" Charlotte mouthed with a smirk. Blushing and without explanation, Magda straightened her skirt.

"My friend came in for her first tattoo," she said with an effort at dignity reclamation. "Holbein, this is—."

"Charlotte," the man finished, eyes twinkling. "And I understand you're here for these, not a tattoo." From under the counter he produced a piece of sketch paper and an envelope, which he handed to Charlotte.

"Thank you, Mr. Holbein," she said. "Now, who tells her?"

"Tells me what?" Magda bounced on the balls of her feet, looking from Holbein to Charlotte like a caffeinated cat watching high-speed tennis.

"She might throttle me," Charlotte drawled, taking a step back. "Why don't you?" "With pleasure, ma'am. Underfoot, stand still now." Magda stilled with an impatient soft snort and a bit of effort. "You told your gentleman Julian about the ink you wanted. He brought in art for it, and, if you find what he brought acceptable, got a gift certificate for you." He slid the piece of sketch paper down the immaculate counter from in front of Charlotte to rest in front of Magda. "Of course you don't have to get it now—or ever. I'd give you the lecture about hasty ink and pressure, but you've always had a good head on your shoulders. I'm just reminding you."

Eyes fixed on the drawing, shining with tears, Magda held up a hand to forestall further disclaimers. "Are you free?"

"Absolutely," the man said.

Two and a half hours later, Magda exited the shop sporting two bandages—one on each forearm in the location a watch face would be. As the tattoo artist reminded her to leave them on for an hour before washing and applying ointment, his own eyes had welled and he insisted on taking a picture of the new artwork. "I'll send you copies," he said.

The uncharacteristic display of sentimentality startled Magda "Holbein, are you okay?"

"You know how I am about what matters," he replied gruffly. She nodded, mystified, and Charlotte surreptitiously wiped an eye herself.

Just before she started the car, Charlotte's phone rang with a call from Julian. "Hello?" she said brightly.

"Charlotte," Julian said, voice tight with nervousness. "Did everything go well?"

She glanced at Magda—stretching in clearly enjoyable response to pain and endorphins—and rolled her eyes. "Now's not the best time. I'm just getting on the road. Why don't you call me at home in an hour or so."

Julian chuckled. "Got it. So you'll be here in about 45 minutes?"

Charlotte considered, and brightened. "I'll ask. One moment." Turning to Magda, she snapped her fingers. "Pause the purr for a moment, sweetie. Can I ask you for a favor?"

"Anything," Magda said, stretching. Julian heard and laughed delightedly, and Charlotte's smile widened.

"Can I put Arnold on your couch for the evening?"

"Punishment?" Concern tightened her features.

"Not at all! A reward, actually. He'll prefer the company at your home to mine this evening, and he's earned it. Do you mind?"

"Not at all," Magda said, extending her arms with a sigh.

"That sounds just fine," Charlotte said, resuming the call.

"Well done," Julian replied admiringly.

"You're welcome! You'll tell me how everything turns out when I see you?"

"We both will, I'm sure," he said wryly. "Drive safe."

"I will! Bye," Charlotte finished, hanging up and tossing her phone in her purse. Then, she turned to Magda. "Let's get you home before you soak my car seat, sweetie."

"Charlotte!"

"Spare me. I can hear you purring. Now, entertain me on the drive to your place."

Magda thought for a moment. "Want to play *After I Die?*"

"Sure. Name a category."

"Music collection," Magda answered.

"Songs or artists?"

She considered. "Songs."

Charlotte nodded. "Hmmm. Songs. Okay. After I die and before anyone can find out I own them, hide my copies of..."

Tossing answers back and forth, they passed the drive quickly. Still, Magda's new ink had started to clear its throat and speak up regarding the inevitability of pain. With fifteen more minutes remaining before the bandages could come off, Magda hugged Charlotte tightly but carefully and scampered up the walk to her door.

Julian greeted her just inside, laughing when she launched herself into his arms. Something in his embrace felt strange but she disregarded it instantly, unable to contain herself. "I can't believe you did that!"

"Did what?" he asked quickly.

Joy naked and shining on her face, she waved her bandages wildly. "What do you think?"

He examined her face, green eyes brightly vivid against the pale skin, smile shining with happiness, and pulled her close. A soft startled grunt of pain escaped him, and she stepped back. "Did you get hurt?"

"Not so much." Inexplicably, he winked. Magda's face went quizzical and kittenish, and he shook his head with a chuckle. "I have an idea."

"Another one? After this last idea of yours, I'm game! Lay it on me," she said, bouncing on her toes again in anticipation.

"We'll see. Let's go sit in the living room." He paused, checking his watch. "Oh, it's been almost an hour! Why don't you go get those bandages off and wash your new ink? I put that soap you used last time in the bathroom. Meet me in the living room for ointment," he added as she trooped off.

"What an offer," she called over her shoulder, shouting throatily.

"You have no idea," Julian muttered to himself, turning towards the other room.

Five minutes later, seated beside Magda on the sofa, Julian said, "Let me see."

Feeling the pain now, Magda extended her arms. Two identical Mobius strips in a rainbow's progressed shades decorated her outer forearms beginning an inch below her wrists. Fresh, they glistened surrounded by the red skin new ink creates. Tentatively, she asked, "Do you like them?"

"More than you know," he said. "You explained what they meant to you. Mind if I repcat it back to you, to make sure I have it straight?"

Perplexed, she tilted her head to one side.

"You said we don't lose anything that matters. The colors may blend and shift, but they stay the same." He paused, holding her hands. "Your mom may not be here anymore, but you haven't lost all of her. And we may have had a crazy off-and-on twenty years, but here we are again. We don't lose all of what matters. You realized that and got it in ink to keep it with you forever. How am I doing so far?"

"Great," she whispered.

"And being half-twisted is what makes the Mobius strip work," he continued slowly. "One strip, half a twist. Trace a line around it and almost by magic it covers both sides to find its way back to the beginning. An amazing thing that wouldn't work if it wasn't a little twisted," he concluded.

"Amazing things often are," Magda said softly.

"Let's get them seen to," Julian said. On cue, Arnold entered the room with a tray bearing antibacterial analgesic ointment, two fingers of single malt scotch, a tall glass of water, and a few napkins. He placed it on the coffee table with a brief smile at Magda and left the room briskly. Julian picked up the ointment and proceeded to smear a thin coating over her new tattoos.

"To me," he said conversationally, "they mean all that and a bit more. It's been a long and twisted trip over the past twenty years. We're not the same people who dated in high school, but here we are."

"Here we are," she echoed, reaching to touch the back of his hand.

"When you make a Mobius strip with a piece of paper, you give it a half twist and tape the two ends together." Gently, he put her hands down. As he continued, he undid the buttons of his shirt cuffs carefully. "Over the two decades we've known each other you've gotten ten tattoos—now twelve—and I've liked looking at them. You know that. I didn't understand the motivation to get them until you talked about getting these, and I thought about what they meant to each of us."

"I love you," she said with an urgency prompted by the solemnity of his manner, picking up his hand and leaning forward to kiss it.

"You'd better," he replied, lips twisting in a wry smile. "Because I'm not done yet." He pulled out the velvet box, this time from a pocket in his slacks, and put it on the couch between them. Magda tensed, silent, as she grasped its possible contents. "Give me a second," he added.

"Take your time," she said weakly, reaching for her scotch.

Julian handed it to her, took a gulp of his water and drew in a deep breath. "For most couples commitment is a risk because they imagine what could go wrong. With us, it's a risk because we remember what already has. At first some things may have been a test—for both of us. Tests to see what we would do, whether or not we would back out, if we could work. We've passed that, though. We're not seeing if we'll work, we're learning how we work best. We just haven't said it outright. And maybe simply saying it isn't enough with us."

Rolling up his sleeves, he revealed a pair of tattoos exactly like hers except fit to scale for his larger forearms. Magda gasped. "I told you what they mean to me. I want to come back to what matters, always. I want to smile at them when I think of you during the day, and to never lose what matters, or lose sight of it."

"I could have decided not to get them!" Aghast, Magda exploded. "Or I could have wanted another design! Or not wanted anyone to have ink exactly like mine!"

"All true," Julian agreed, "and all risks. But it's not a test anymore. I would have kept them if you'd decided not to get them or chosen another design. I admit, I didn't consider the unique ink angle, but if it's an issue we'll figure out how to handle it. We're not a test. We're us. And risks for us are worth it."

"It's not an issue," she protested. "Not at all."

"And now I'm saying it." He picked up the box and held it out to her. "With actions and words."

Shocked now to speechlessness, Magda opened the box to find an utterly unique set of rings. Two heavy titanium Mobius strips rested side by side. Above the left one sat another ring, a thick and wide titanium band bearing a ruby. An etched design of a phoenix circled the ring, flames forming the setting for the gemstone.

"Magda, will you marry me?"

Powerful thoughts crossed her mind: their agonizing worst moments over the years, their best ones, their individual strengths and weaknesses. Anticipation of this moment lessened the sting for him of seeing recollected wounds. Nothing could have prepared him for seeing the best of their time together fill the features of her face: affection, amusement, heat, hope, and love warmed her cheeks and moistened her eyes. She raised them to meet his.

"Yes, I will."

Julian picked up a napkin from the tray and wiped ointment residue from his hands before removing the ruby engagement ring from the case. He slid it onto her ring finger and looked at their hands, entirely out of words. He'd seen their hands together before, but never like this. And their new tattoos conferred upon him a temporary gift that stunned him to his foundations. In this singular thing they now shared permanently, he now knew exactly how she felt. He know how the needle had burned, he recalled how the adrenaline had mitigated the pain. He knew how her arms burned at this very moment. He knew precisely what she was going through.

Magda gently freed one hand to wipe tears from his face with her thumb. She hesitated, as though stopping herself from doing something socially unacceptable, and then brought it to her lips to taste his tears.

"Oh, really?" he asked, eyebrows rising.

"It's what I do," she replied.

"You don't have to," Julian said. "It's not a test."

"No, it's not." She smiled, an unburdened happy expression. "It's us. And I want to be all of me with all of you." A tiny frown creased her features. "Not a test, but still a learning curve. Everything won't change or be perfect overnight."

He nodded. "Some things won't ever change. I'm not a slave." She giggled at the idea, and he grinned. "And you like that about me. I'll only submit to you, and only sometimes. Getting better at things together—trials and errors and all—isn't the bad part, love. It's the good part. 'Even better' gives us more to look forward to."

At that second the doorbell rang, heavy church bells in deference to Magda's fear of ever missing a knock. The couple heard Arnold's soft footsteps as he swiftly answered it, the sound of something large changing hands, and some friendly banter before the door closed again.

Curious, the couple looked up to watch Arnold bring a large box into the room with the help of an adorable plump brunette in her early twenties. The pair exchanged a few words in conspiratorial undertones regarding placement before setting it down opposite the couch. Pointing at the box, she whispered something to Arnold, who nodded.

Magda cleared her throat sharply, causing both Julian and the new arrival to jump. "Arnold, you haven't introduced my new guest."

Julian's head snapped to look at his girlfriend—now fiancée—in shock. Arnold, however, straightened infinitesimally. The brief inclination of his head conveyed both acknowledgment and apology. "Please forgive me, Ma'am. I should have introduced her immediately, and regret my lack of manners. If any opportunity arises for me to make amends, I bet you to permit me the chance to do so."

Magda nodded. The girl stepped forward to introduce herself, but Arnold stopped her with a soft smack to the back of the head, and Julian observed as his beloved forced a snicker into a stern expression.

"Ma'am, please allow me to introduce Natalie. She belongs to Coleen O'Reilly and Sophia Marsh. Natalie, this is Magda Kasden and," Arnold paused, smiling, "her fiancé, Julian."

"I'm pleased to meet you, ma'am." Natalie bowed gracefully and deeply from the neck and shoulders. "I had the honor of meeting your aunt, and she spoke very highly of you."

"Thank you," Magda replied. Observing Natalie's uncertain body language, she added, "I believe your owners expect you back at Charlotte's shortly."

The slave blinked in surprise at the correct deduction, but she recovered to respond smoothly. "Just as you say, ma'am."

"Then Arnold must see you to the door." At her words, Arnold extended an arm and led Natalie to the door. As they waited for him to return, Julian watched Magda's face appreciatively. For her part, she examined the box avidly, hands smoothing her skirt the way a curious cat smooths carpet with a waving tail. Her stare snapped to Arnold the moment he re-entered the room. "Arnold?"

"Getting the explanation for you, Ma'am," he said. Opening the unsealed box but obstructing Magda's view deliberately, he removed a heavy ivory envelope and passed it to her.

She opened it with the knife he proffered in anticipation of her requirement and pulled out a folded page of thick, creamy parchment. The first sentence rendered her insensible to all other sounds in the room.

My beloved Mugwump,

By now you've become my beloved engaged Mugwump. From the moment you found yourself single nearly a year ago I resolved to find a way to give you one of these, and I intended to give this to you on your birthday. However, while it now seems like the proverbial coals to Newcastle, please accept it as my engagement present.

Also, please accept Arnold's service this evening if you like. Give Julian his chance to give you that evidence, sweetie. As to Arnold's behavioral status, he is most certainly not being punished. I believe you will agree he did a fine job designing your new tattoos.

I couldn't be more proud... of us all.

Love,

Charlotte

Eyes watering freely, Magda passed the letter to Julian—and blinked at the space where the box had been. In its place on an oversized burgundy pillow facing the couch sat the saddle-shaped base of a device covered in black leather. The cord for the controls stretched to the coffee table where Arnold had placed them, and where anyone on either the device or the couch could easily reach them.

Julian tore his eyes from the device to read the letter. "Is that the thing we saw..." Julian asked, question trailing off as he considered.

"Yes!" she squealed. "That video! Charlotte showed it to me, and let me borrow the DVD to show to you. And then," she grinned, "you found those other videos to show me."

He smiled wickedly. "Now I recall. All I had to do was look up 'Sybian'. It does seem to be missing something though," Julian added, inspecting it.

"Pardon me," said Arnold as he re-entered the room. "I'm

seeing to that now." Efficiently he snapped a rosy pink rectangular silicon attachment onto the center of the foot-long base. First he attached the rear snaps, one hand on the raised ridge while the other connected the snaps. He repeated the process in front, this time with one hand holding a ridge covered in a texture of small, soft nubs. Ensuring he'd affixed it securely, he examined the item between the ridges. With his fingers around the shaft, he cupped the bulb on its end and pulled gently. Satisfied he'd properly secured the attachment as a whole, he reached for the control box on the table.

Arnold turned one of the two dials on the box slowly to the maximum setting and nodded to himself at the clearly audible and palpable vibrations. A muted chuckle emerged from Julian and he said appreciatively, "That seems almost excessive." As the vibrations continued, Arnold repeated the process with the second dial. The bulbed protrusion began to rotate in small concentric circles, the speed increasing. Magda's lips parted. When both functions reached their highest settings, Arnold observed the device for about fifteen seconds to confirm the base remained in place. Assembly and testing complete, he turned off the machine and returned the control box to the coffee table.

Julian set down the letter and faced Magda.

"Thoughts, love?"

"Coals to Newcastle indeed," she said, wiping her eyes. "As though we weren't already lucky enough, in every way."

He cupped her face in his hands and kissed her thoroughly. "Actually, I believe there's one more way. Something you wanted to see."

Julian stood, fastening his shirt cuffs, and addressed the slave. "Arnold, strip and show yourself."

Arnold removed his clothing and stacked it out of the way in a neat pile. In graceful silence he faced both of them, legs slightly spread and fingers laced behind his head. The posture flattered the slave's minimal muscle definition, bringing a hint of shadow to the outlines of his calves and quadriceps. Dignity and something ineffable elevated the rather nondescript man's appearance to a riveting one. "Next," Julian ordered, prompting Arnold to swivel smoothly and reveal his back. The repeated command brought the slave through two more positions coming to rest on his knees facing the couple. Spine straight, hands resting lightly on his thighs, he awaited further instruction with alert calm.

From the command to present, Magda had watched Julian with wide eyes. Now she stood and approached her former trainee, tilting his chin up with a finger. "The designs are lovely," she said. "Thank you."

"It is an honor to be of service," Arnold replied. His perfect posture broke so minutely no one other than his former trainer or his owner would have noticed it, let alone recognized its significance—a knee injury that merely caused physical discomfort. The mental irritation of deviation from perfect service, however, bothered the exemplary slave to no end.

"Well done," she said. "Take a seat on the couch, Arnold."

He rose and moved to obey, but before he could sit Julian said, "No, Arnold. I'd prefer if you lay down."

Magda, about to reclaim her seat, looked at Julian quizzically.

As Arnold complied with the last order given, Julian answered her look. "I just wanted to give you a better view, love." Bemused, Magda stepped away from the couch and sat on the floor next to the Sybian, curling her legs under her as the slave stretched out.

Julian approached Arnold, put a hand on his outward knee and splayed his legs. Julian took advantage of the newly created space to seat himself, while reaching to caress the slave's freshly shaved scrotum. He cupped it gently, and then drew his hand up to feel softly along Arnold's erect shaft.

Shifting his gaze to Magda, he cracked an involuntary smile at the sight of her. Hand up her shirt, she squeezed her left nipple with her right hand. Her eyes met his with heated anticipation, and he calculated his next action.

A quick gasp emerged from Arnold as Julian's hand contracted. Magda's hand echoed the motion, and with a moue of impatience she stripped off her tank top and the bra underneath. Swiftly one hand returned to the glint of revealed metal piercing her nipple, the other caressing her upper chest.

She watched avidly as Julian's lips enclosed the head of the slave's cock and then immediately pulled away. Rather than continue with his mouth, he ran a merciless grip over the now-slick sensitive skin. Her fingers slid under her waistband of her skirt just as a low moan escaped Arnold, and she stood to simply remove her remaining clothes.

Under the weight of two pairs of eyes, she unbuttoned her skirt and pushed it and her panties to the floor. Magda's trimmed shock of red pubic hair stood out starkly against the background of white skin. Her curvy petite milkmaid figure seemed incongruously wholesome, given the brightly colored tattoos and nipple piercings. With the impeccable sense of timing she'd always enjoyed, Arnold's lips curved appreciatively and a wave of mischief possessed her.

Wielding the eye contact like a whip, she glared at him. "You should not have permitted anyone into my home without a proper introduction, Arnold. You know better." The slave opened his mouth to apologize and she cut him off with a gesture. "Yes, you deserve a reward... but you didn't think that mistake would go uncorrected, did you? Of course not." She smiled malevolently. "Don't you dare blow your load until I tell you that you may. One second sooner and I'll send your ass back to Charlotte with so many stripes she'll mistake you for a fucking trainee. Say the words."

"Not until you say, Ma'am," he responded sharply.

Taking advantage of the new status quo, Julian chuckled to himself and began to tease Arnold in earnest. Deliberately he wrapped his mouth around the cock in his hand, lips following his strokes, fully aware the slave would fight with all the control he could muster to obey any order from his former trainer.

Arnold's eyes closed. Still staying—and unable to tear her gaze away—Magda watched Julian. His actions shattered every spiteful automatic stereotype about the demeaning and submissive nature of giving head. She thought he looked glorious, taking the slave's submission and dictating how much pleasure he would permit. The warmth between her thighs turned to heat as she watched Julian's iron forearms move and the muscles in his shoulders bunch under the skin. As the heat turned to throbbing, she took a deep breath and lowered her head... to the Sybian.

Between the scene before her and her curiosity about the device, it took less than a second for her to decide to try it. Magda squirted a bit of the lube Arnold had set down behind the base onto the bulb, and she spread the liquid down the shaft. Settling her knees on the pillow astride the device, she lowered herself down onto it and sighed as the bulb slid all the way in. After some shifting to find her balance she reached for the control box.

The mildest vibrations drove the nubs into her throbbing clit like electricity itself, and Magda moaned. Arnold echoed her and she snapped, "Say the words, boy."

Between gritted teeth Arnold replied, "Not until you say, Ma'am."

Nodding, she turned the dial. The rear ridge thrummed against her ass, the bulb tickled her G-spot with increasing force and its shaft buzzed against her inner lips. She rode the machine lightly at first, but ground down on it involuntarily at the sight of Julian sliding a finger into Arnold's mouth. Magda turned the dial controlling the shaft and bulb's rotation, and soon a raw sound drew the attention of the men on the couch.

A deep flush coloring her chest, Magda arched her back as her fingers gripped the front of the Sybian. Not all orgasms are created alike; the onset of more than one kind contorted the woman. Her clit warred with itself, at once grinding against and backing away from the nubs. Her abdomen rippled with the force of internal contractions caused by the twists against her G-spot. A sheen of sweat coated her skin as everything narrowed to the force of the orgasm on the horizon.

"Now, Arnold," she growled, still watching with lids narrowed.

At her words, Julian withdrew his lips. His hand kept working the slave's cock, concentrating on the head with his thumb and fingers. With a spasm Arnold began to obediently come, and Julian shifted his hand to firmly stroke only the shaft. Arnold groaned loudly, and both the sight and sound pushed Magda over the edge.

She leaned forward to seize the edge of the coffee table as the force of the orgasm struck her. Coming in waves, her head dropped as the rest of her body went rigid. She groaned, a raw and ragged sound torn from her throat as she shook from shoulders to pelvis. It took a moment for her to be able to even reach for the control box, but at last she finally managed to turn the machine off.

It took some moments until Magda rose just enough to extricate herself, tipping over and trying to catch her breath. Observing the soaked device, she chuckled. "That's going to require some cleanup."

Arnold got to his feet immediately, collecting the device and removing it from the room. Magda stood and walked around the table to meet Julian, who had also risen. "I've always wanted to see that," she said.

"I know, love," he replied.

His arms moved to circle her waist as hers wrapped around his neck, and they kissed, embracing. As he stepped away, however, her hands moved to press firmly on his shoulders. His face reflected confusion, and he raised an eyebrow.

Smiling, she began to push him down towards the couch until he was lying on his back. "Oh, no," Magda said, shaking her head. "We're not finished yet, my dear." A wry smile appeared on Julian's face at her words, his heart warming at the endearment.

As she straddled Julian's head and he flicked her clit lightly with his tongue, he murmured, "Only us." His tongue flitted across the spot a few more times before he added, "You know I love you."

She lowered herself even further down and between gasps said, "You'd better."

Foreword

What else should follow a story of love and marriage and happy, device-aided three-way sex than a terrifying glimpse into yet another nightmare of slavery? In the Marketplace, it's understood that slaves cannot dictate who may own them and for what purposes, except in a narrow range of contracted limits. Plus, the more limits a contract includes, the less desirable the property becomes. (This is where fantasy becomes useful, of course.) Assuming a world where the owners are not outright abusive still leaves many unhappy possibilities when matching strangers. The most obvious bad sale scenario is when the owner does not fit the physical or orientation preferences of the slave; too old, too young, not big, too small, too liberal, too religious... and of course, the worst fate of all, "not interested in sex or play with the slave."

Or, is that really the worst?

What if the slave doesn't even understand what the owner wants?

At all?

S. M. Li was born in Malaysia and grew up in Kota Kinabalu and Hong Kong before emigrating to the U.S. in 1996. Laura Antoniou's Marketplace series and other writings have been an inspiration to her for more than a decade. She has served as an editor for the PoetryNet and Literotica websites, and her poetry has appeared in the *Charles River Review*. If she could magically attain mad skills in any writing style she wanted, she'd choose Jane Austen meets Sylvia Plath, only naughtier. She currently lives in Boston with her owner, her dogs, and her puppyboy.

Getting Real
S.M. Li

"She wants to know if they taught you how to suffer."

Oliver licks his lips, tastes salted breath. He mouths the familiar sounds that feel alien here among the alienating chatter that has surrounded him the entire trip. Didn't "She" speak English? Why buy a slave who can't speak your language? Japanese? No. Chinese? It didn't matter. He doesn't know either one.

"I—" He winces at the dry crack in his voice, wonders again what possessed him to decline his Trainer's offer to match him with an Owner. *"I know several people who would be just right for you, Oliver. I'm going to visit one of them next month. Once I show him how beautifully he can handle you, he'll buy you on the spot."*

But he hadn't wanted to do it the Geoff Negel way. That felt too easy, too planned and negotiated, too much like the Soft World he'd spent years trying to rise above—or perhaps sink below. "Thank you, sir, but I would prefer to take my chances at auction," he'd said. Yes, he understood that meant his Trainer would have no control over who bought him—of course; but that was the point. *That would make it real.*

Oliver hadn't dared say out loud the last part.

Now he isn't even sure what it means. He's been hours inside this airline kennel—hours waiting, hours wondering where he is, hours willing himself to patience. Every now and then someone had come to take him out—bare minutes of exquisite freedom to relieve his cramped muscles and bladder—but nobody's spoken to him until now. During those long, tedious hours, his thoughts had lurched back and forth between fantasy and fear. His cock had done the same.

Hearing his Trainer's name and his own woven into the undecipherable knots of foreign speech trading over his head, Oliver's chest fills with rocky misery. Surely they think him a poorly trained slave, not even capable of answering a simple question. The translator's voice is low and deferential, and Oliver wonders if the man is a slave, too. *Probably one of those uber-perfect ones who never misstep or misspeak,* he thinks.

"Perfect is boring. Perfect doesn't give you anything to punish, and what's the fun in that?" He'd always laughed when someone said that—laughed and nodded—but now he's not so sure about it. Now he's finding himself not sure about a lot of things.

The man leans down and peers through the wire-mesh door. Aviator-style sunglasses reflect Oliver's own wide-eyed gaze back at him. He smiles suddenly, displaying a mouthful of flawless white teeth. "Do you neglect to answer, Oliver?"

Startled, scrambling for an adequate response, he blurts, "Please, sir. I don't—"

A sharp thump on the kennel roof informs him those particular words are unacceptable. He wants to try again, but falters in his fatigue, discouraged, disoriented by the long journey nobody bothered to explain to him. They'd just crated him up after the auction, the stoic staff at first answering his queries with smiles and shrugs, and *You'll-find-out-later's,* then later ignoring them. Dread seizes him for several stretched seconds. Will they send him back to Geoff? Kick him out of the Marketplace for being a spectacular failure? He trips over his own hesitation and gives up trying to speak, huddling down with a contrite moan.

Laughter. Then, a woman's low, mocking, faux-sympathetic, "Ohhh." He doesn't know which is worse: the sinking, twisting tension in his gut or the rising, twitching arousal between his legs. "Oliver." She pronounces his name with a softened L, rolling the sound into a gentle R, her voice quiet, almost coaxing.

He raises his head, at once reassured and uneasy by how gently she speaks to him. How many times during his training had he been sweet-talked into relaxing his diligence, only to stumble into swift, sudden trouble? He is determined not to make the same mistake here. Slender legs, small feet in glossy red pumps, move in front of the doorway. The wire-mesh panel swings open.

"Oliver." Same inflection, but louder now, the last syllable drawn up and out.

"*Owners want responsive, obedient slaves,*" his Spotter used to say. "*They don't want to wait around while you work through your shit. Do what you're told, when you're told.*" It had all seemed to make perfect sense at the time.

Unsure of what to do, but sure that saying so would not be met with approval, Oliver lets out a pleading little moan. Hearing himself, he winces. He hates how pathetic he sounds.

More laughter. Footsteps moving away—heels clicking on concrete—then: snapping fingers; a long, two-toned whistle; clapping hands.

More than anything, Oliver wishes for someone to just tell him what to do, in words he can understand. He feels utterly unprepared for this, as though his months in training were all for naught. In his confusion, he tries the only thing that comes to mind. Tucking his knees tightly beneath his body, he prostrates himself, reaching his hands, palm-down, out in front. "This slave begs your forgiv—"

"Bù!"

Her meaning is unmistakable. Choking back the formal apology, he pushes up onto his elbows and slumps against the side of the crate.

"Oliver." She whistles. "Oliver, *guò lai.*"

The unfamiliar syllables taunt him. He looks up slowly, half expecting to be smacked over the head for not keeping his eyes down, and blinks at the sight of a petite Asian woman sitting cross-legged on the floor several feet from him. Oliver can't help himself: his eyes linger on her face, where pale, pale pink cherry blossoms—drawn or tattooed, he can't tell, though their exquisite detail suggests the latter—start over the right cheekbone and curve delicately down her jaw and neck to disappear under her shirt. He can't help himself: he stares. Her smile admonishes him, and he looks down in a hurry, flushing at his own lack of control.

"Guò lai," she calls softly, gesturing for him to approach.

Oliver crawls out of the crate onto the cool floor. His traitorous cock is hard again, its stiff, hanging weight serving only to heighten the dread and humiliation of being so naked, stripped bare of both clothes and language, with strangers seemingly intent on treating him like some dumb beast. They'd shipped him here in a dog crate, for God's sake!

She unlocks and removes his chain collar, replacing it with a wide leather one that closes with a metal buckle. Then she hooks a finger through the D-ring and yanks his head up. Oliver has barely a second to register the smile in her eyes before she slaps him hard across his left cheek. He gasps, and she slaps him again. And again. His eyes struggle to focus, making the cherry blossoms on her face look like they are falling.

The tumbling chimes of a doorbell reach them, faint but insistent. She ignores it, but the man, who Oliver still hasn't gotten a good look at, walks past them and leaves the room, presumably to answer the summons. For the first time, Oliver notices that they are in a garage; to his right is a dark-blue Mercedes sedan, the curve of its gleaming door distorting his image as though reflecting how he feels inside. The bare walls peak high into a vaulted ceiling, their flat grey surfaces adorned with neither window nor color.

He hears a shrill female voice raised in excited greeting. The owner of the voice fairly bounces into the room, teetering slightly on wicked high heels, ribbons and ruffled petticoats swishing about her legs in a froth of black tulle and silk brocade. *Steampunk goes to China,* Oliver thinks, while a vague fantasy of being ordered under those abundant petticoats flits through his mind. A sharp yank on the collar, fierce enough to force his head down, tells him he's been caught staring again. He blushes, biting back a groan.

Abruptly releasing her hold, his tormentor gets to her feet, rising out of her seated position in a fluid dancer's move. Oliver stays where she's left him. Even on his hands and knees, he feels the contrast of his own unwieldy size and gracelessness keenly. Though of average height and build, next to her, he feels like a lumbering giant.

❦

"*Tā shì hǎo kàn, shì bù shì?*" she asks, without turning to greet her visitor, who arrives in a flounce of skirt and squeals.

"Wang Fei-Ying! I cannot believe you actually went and bought one! Sure, he's good-looking, but what use is good-looking if not properly trained?"

"Oh, Xiao-Chun, I have enough useful slaves. Have you seen my newest from Noguchi? She does everything. Anyway, this one's for fun."

The woman glances down at the trembling man. "Ying, the poor creature is terrified. What have you been doing to him?"

Ying smiles. "Just playing while I waited for you. If he is terrified, it is probably because he doesn't understand anything anyone is saying."

Her friend rolls her eyes. "Playing, yes. I can see evidence of your 'playing' here." She indicates Oliver's reddened cheek. "And here." Extending her foot under his body, she aims a light kick at the man's still-hard cock. He flinches, but makes no sound. Xiao-Chun grins. "Maybe he is thinking that this is a dream come true—under the control of 'beautiful'—she holds up her hands and mimes quotes around her next word—'Oriental' women who will be deliciously cruel to him. Isn't that what the American men like?"

Now it is Ying's turn to roll her eyes. "You've been looking at too much porn. Besides, this one is from England."

"But he trained at that place in California you told me about, right?"

"Yes, and—"

"I still can't believe you gave good money to a place you said made slaves no better than dogs!"

Ying gives a dismissive wave. "It was not such good money. And I didn't say that: I said they made slaves that are like *puppies*. You know, mostly cute and fun, but with no care for proper behavior."

"If you wanted a puppy, you should've gotten one of those

Canadian ones. I hear they're marvelously trained."

"They are! A friend of mine has a pair. Two boys. Very committed and beautiful, but also kind of limited."

Xiao-Chun eyes the slave at their feet. "And he's not?"

"He is, but only because he thinks he is something," Ying murmurs, fingers lightly scratching the shivering Oliver's back. "When he realizes he is not...." she trails off into a theatrical sigh.

Xiao-Chun gives her friend a questioning look.

Ying digs her nails into the skin beneath her fingertips. "They come so soft, so sure of their worth. Of course, they are taught to take beatings and to do the unpleasant chores, and to smile and like it; they are taught to be pleasing for sex and to be obedient in service; but they are not taught to suffer—*to give.*"

Oliver tries to pay attention to the tangled tones of their rapid conversation, but it's no use. He's hungry and tired, his knees hurt, the nails in his back are driving him crazy, his balls ache, and his cock is starting to feel schizophrenic.

The petticoat woman crouches down, balancing with impressive nonchalance on those excruciating heels, and cups a hand under his chin, pulling it forward and forcing him to look into her eyes. Finger and thumb press uncomfortably beneath his jaw, pinching the top of his trachea. Reflexively, he swallows; he is intensely aware of how his throat flutters against her hand when he does that, and wants desperately to look away, but she holds him there while her other hand reaches under his body.

Warm fingers circle the base of his cock, squeezing balls against shaft. Oliver feels himself harden almost instantly, as though the nerves in his groin just woke up all at once. He sucks in a breath. "Oh God," he blurts, his voice scaling up sharply.

The woman laughs. She lets go of him, and stands up. "Zuò xia," she says, her eyes expectant.

Oliver stares up at her, miserable in his ignorance.

She stabs him with a stern look. "Zuò," she says, then, again, much louder, "ZUÒ."

And all he can do is wait for the correcting hand that grabs the back of his collar and drags him up and back to sit on his heels.

"Bèn-dàn," Xiao-Chun mutters.

Ying laughs, shaking her head. "He's not. He has no idea what you're saying." She pokes her friend in the arm, teasing, "Saying it louder won't magically make it make sense to him."

"Pah!" Xiao-Chun scowls. "Why didn't you buy one who knows even a *little* Mandarin?" She sets a booted foot on top of the slave's left thigh, angling the stiletto heel over his retreating cock. "Or how to stay hard?" Oliver lets out a panicky squeak as she shifts her weight, and she grins.

Ying tsks, wagging a finger at her friend, mock-scolding, "Don't break my new toy!"

Wobbling a little on her one precarious heel, Xiao-Chun moves her foot higher, onto Oliver's lower belly, and leans forward until she sees his muscles jump in reaction. "Maybe your new puppy needs to go shi-shi," she asks, directing her mocking singsong at the jittery slave. "Isn't that what dogs do? Pee on themselves to show their submission?" She shoves her boot harder into his abdomen.

Ying presses a hand over Oliver's forehead, forcing him to lean back and give her his eyes. "Have your fun," she says softly, tracing light fingers from temple to jaw, opening his mouth. She runs the pad of her thumb along the top of his lower teeth. "But just bear in mind that if you hurt him too much, it will only help him."

"Help him?"

She smiles down at the shaking man. "Physical suffering is easy. You wait. You endure. Then it is done. And all the while, you are distracted from the good stuff going on in here." She taps a finger against the side of Oliver's head.

Xiao-Chun pushes off the sweet spot over his bladder, making him groan, and stamps her foot onto the ground between his knees. Oliver winces. "Ying, I didn't come here to listen to your philosophies. I want to have some fun!"

"We're already having fun."

"What? He's failing everything!"

Ying frames Oliver's face with her hands. "Look into his eyes. You think he's not giving us anything? Just look—it's delicious." She leans down, close, as though she's about to kiss him, then, just as suddenly, releases him and steps back. "He's not ready, though. Not yet."

They leave him alone after that, for what feels like hours. He spends most of the time trying to convince himself that this is a test, that she's not really going to kick him around like some cowering pet for the next year. Surely she has some actual *use* for him, some *real* purpose? There's nothing in his contract to stop her from keeping him in the goddamn garage and feeding him table scraps for the next three-hundred-and-sixty-five days, but what was the fucking point? Oliver's frantic thoughts reel and wring him through a hundred unwelcome what-ifs. He is no stranger to animal role-play—he's played the puppy for male and female lovers alike, and romped happily with other slaves during training—but that was playing; those were games; this is...

"Safeword; fucking safeword!" he whispers fiercely to himself, fighting the tears that threaten to erode what shreds of composure he has left. But there are no safewords here, no outs save complete separation from the Marketplace, and that he cannot bear to even imagine. He's still struggling with it when he falls to exhausted sleep.

The sound of metal scraping on concrete drags him awake. He heaves open his eyes; they feel gritty, tired still. Someone is pulling a chair across the floor. Someone—

Her voice sings out, "Oliver!"

He jerks upright, eyes wide open.

"*Guò lái.*"

Oliver hesitates for just a second before rolling onto his hands and knees, and crawling to where she sits, legs crossed left over right at the knee. He is relieved to see that she is alone, the petticoat woman nowhere in sight or sound. Her feet are bare, and when he gets close, he sees that her left foot and leg are tattooed—he can see that now—like her face, the elegant flowers continuing their poetry from knee to ankle to sole.

"Oliver, *zuò.*"

He promptly sits back on his heels, sighing a little with relief that he can actually understand and carry out an order. His heart sinks when he hears her disapproving tsk-tsk, and looks up to see her pointedly shaking her head at his soft cock. He flushes, mind launching into every trick he has ever learned or even just heard of to produce an erection. Nothing. *Nothing.* Oliver wants to weep in frustration.

She snaps her fingers. Oliver jerks his gaze to her hand. Fingers forming a V, pointing at her eyes, clearly say, *Look at me.* He lets her lock his gaze to hers, holding his breath when he feels the top of her foot against his balls. She makes a quiet exclamation, something that sounds like, "uh oh," and Oliver feels her smile before he even sees it, before he feels her brusquely jam her toes up against his perineum. His cock surges as though she'd kicked it into gear.

She laughs, producing a small bone-shaped dog toy from her pocket and dangling it in front of him. He stares at it, knowing exactly what she's going to do and willing himself to believe that she won't do it—but of course she does. The bone bounces against the far wall, tumbling to the ground with a little thump. She points at it, and snaps her fingers. Oliver, head hanging, crawls over and picks it up in his mouth, biting down furiously on the foul-tasting bone as he returns to his position at her feet. This feels completely stupid and useless, not at all the kind of submission he thought the Marketplace would give him, not—

"Oliver," she says, her voice both question and warning.

Fuck. He's lost his erection. Tense seconds follow, as he desperately tries to get it back, but, again, nothing. She sighs, takes the toy from his mouth, and slaps him across the face. Then she reaches down and whacks his wayward cock with the rubber bone. Oliver yelps, getting the message loud and clear. He can't do it, though—can't get hard, can't stay hard, can't please her, just *can't.* He loses track of how many times she tosses the bone across the room. He just keeps crawling and fetching until his knees start to bleed, tracking narrow smears of blood on the floor between her chair and the far wall.

Finally, she flings the toy into the dog crate, and Oliver creeps inside after it, his soft, sore cock dangling between his legs like a tucked tail. She slams shut the door, leaning down to deliver a harsh scolding that Oliver understands perfectly well even though he has no idea what the words actually mean. Wincing over his scraped, bloody knees, he moves into the back of the kennel, turning his face to the wall and missing the pleased smile she takes with her out of the room.

Oliver stares at the grubby plastic. His knees hurt, but he can't bring himself to care right now. *I'm a fuck up,* he thinks. *I can't get anything right. I can't even get 'just do what you're told' right, because I don't know what the fuck they're telling me.* He punches the wall, trying to stave off the urge to howl with frustration. *My training was a fuck up, a joke. I thought I trained at a good house, but... I don't know. I don't know anything anymore.*

Oliver closes his eyes. His heart is hammering in his chest. He knows there has to be some way to salvage this. There has to be! He feels tears starting, and scrubs furiously at his eyes, as though he can scour away his failures. *But they set me up to fail! This isn't what I expected. I thought—I thought...* He lets out a growl, pressing his palms to his eyes. *I'm stupid. I'm stupid and I'm a fuck up. What did I expect? I wanted* it to be real, and if this isn't mother-getting-fucking real! Oliver almost laughs—feels the hysterical giggle in his chest—and savagely smashes the urge back down.

It's not about you, Oliver snarls at himself. *Everything they told you about how you're just as important, because Owners can't be Owners without Slaves, blah blah blah, that's all bullshit. It's. Not. About. You.* "It's about her," he whispers. "About giving her what she wants. What. She. Wants!" His cock stirs, stiffens slowly into a painful erection. *Motherfucking real!* he thinks, and this time, lets himself laugh out loud, and so, too, the tears they come.

Ying hums quietly to herself as she enters the garage, bowl of water in one hand. A low, shaky whine comes from the kennel. She swings open the door. "Oliver," she calls, gently drawing out the sound of his name.

The slave pokes his head out of the crate and looks up at her. He hesitates, a flicker of uncertainty crossing his face, but then seems to visibly commit himself, squaring his shoulders and crawling out before her.

She sets down the bowl. He looks at it, then back at her. Slowly, he sits back on his heels. Another moment of hesitation, then his cupped hands come up to his chest in the stereotypical begging-puppy position, and he starts to mimic a dog's excited panting. It looks so comical she almost bursts out laughing, but instead she reaches down and grasps his hard cock.

"Good boy," she says, enunciating the words slowly even though she knows he doesn't understand. His eyes light up at her tone—for some things, actual words don't matter. She smiles. "You're ready now."

I saved the longest story for last. Not merely because it's long, but because this is a multi-part action-adventure story in the fashion of a classic Victorian "travels abroad" sort of tale. The kind of thing a reader might want to set aside for enjoying over a pot of tea or before bedtime, allowing the setting to carry them away. I like long stories; both to read and write, because I'm the type of reader who wants to be taken along for the journey. And while the characters in this piece travel far—indeed, perhaps a bit too far, where one is concerned—the melodramatic dangers and feats of love, loyalty and derring-do create a picture of a Marketplace not only in an earlier time, but a sepia-colored age of passion, romance, and danger. To have tried to make this contemporary would have made it a farce, as it includes time honored tropes such as improbable coincidences and a quite hardy character enduring suspiciously extreme conditions and non-consensual violence. (Fair warning!) But like most stories of the time, all is sorted out and the lovers rejoice as order is restored. How could I resist this? It's an affectionate tribute to one of my favorite types of naughty writing.

Elizabeth Schechter is a stay-at-home-mom who lives in Central Florida, where she enjoys seeing the looks on the faces of the other playgroup moms when she answers the question "What do you do?" by describing herself as a pervy fetish writer. Her first novel, *Princes of Air*, was published in 2011 by Circlet Press, and her second, a steampunk novel entitled *House of the Sable Locks*, is forthcoming. Elizabeth can be found online at http://easchechter.wordpress.com/

O, Promise Me!
Elizabeth Schechter

The pre-breakfast summons was a mystery—to join the Trainer in her parlor immediately. Thomas wondered why he was being ordered from his usual duties below-stairs, especially so early in the morning, but he also knew the price of both disobedience and dawdling; he put away his cleaning cloths and his apron, rinsed lamp oil, kerosene, and rottenstone from his hands and put on his coat.

"I'll finish the lamps, Mister Carey," said one of the footmen, a nice young Irish lad who was coming along nicely. "I've already laid the table."

"Thank you, Colin," Thomas answered, already heading for the stairs. Outside the parlor door, Thomas paused by the hallway looking glass, making certain of his appearance, and that his collar fell just so. Lady Margaret was particular about the appearance of her personal slaves as well as that the slave-trainers who worked in her house, and it would not do to appear at anything less than his best. If only he could do something about the lingering scent of kerosene! Thomas grimaced slightly, reminded himself that he would need to stand away from the open windows, and knocked on the door.

"Enter," a pleasant female voice called from inside. Thomas opened the door and slipped in, stopping three steps inside the room and bowing slightly.

"My lady?" he said softly. "How may I be of service?" He didn't raise his eyes; instead, he listened, the way he'd been taught. A soft rustle of a day gown—that was Lady Margaret, always dressed to the highest mode. And raspy breathing? That was most definitely not Lady Margaret. No one had spent the night, so someone had arrived very early.

"Thomas, come and join us," Lady Margaret said. "We have

something to discuss with you." Thomas bowed again and crossed the room to Lady Margaret's usual chair, but as he went to kneel next to her, she stopped him. "No, my dear. Take a seat."

Thomas was unable to hide his surprise—he was being allowed furniture? He looked up, seeing both Lady Margaret and her visitor for the first time. Lady Margaret, as always, looked cool and lovely in her pale blue day gown. Her visitor was an older man, dressed all in dark gray and black. Thomas knew him as someone from the Marketplace. He held in his hands a file, one with Thomas' name inscribed on the front. Confused, and trying hard not to show it, Thomas sat down in the chair Lady Margaret indicated and waited.

"Thomas Carey," Lady Margaret said. "Actual name, Thomas Carruthers. Fourth son of the late John Carruthers, Earl of Dunwich, and one of my more promising trainees. His bloodlines are impeccable, and I believe that he will serve nicely to solve your current problems."

The man looked appraisingly at Thomas, and then cleared his throat. "He's presentable enough to please her. Tell me, boy, how does a member of the peerage end up in a collar?"

Thomas bowed his head. "As my lady says, I am the fourth son, and the youngest of seven children. Dunwich was never a large estate, and if you know the peerage, my lord, you know of my father and his... habits."

"I know that your father was... unwell, for quite some time."

Thomas smiled slightly. "Thank you, sir, for your kindness, but the truth is well known. My father was a drunkard, and a great deal of Dunwich disappeared into his cups. When he passed, we were forced to sell off a majority of the land in order to pay debts. All that is left is the entailment. Add to that the dowries for three sisters, and the cost of two brothers in the Royal Navy, and you can see that there was little left in Dunwich to offer the youngest son. I have not the temperament for the Royal Navy, nor a calling to clergy, so I entered service. " He paused and looked fondly at Lady Margaret. "In time, I'll be a Master-Trainer, or so my lady tells me. I will finish my time as a journeyman after the new year."

The man hummed thoughtfully. "Yes... Margaret, I think he will do."

"Thomas," Lady Margaret said. "This is James Stafford, Baron Waterton. As you may have guessed, he is an Owner, and he is facing a unique problem."

"The problem is that my son and heir, Sebastian, died a year ago," Stafford explained. "Under the law, my daughter Eugenia cannot hold Waterton. I must see her wed, to save my lands and the people under my care." Stafford sighed and looked at Thomas. "Whoever my Ginny marries must be of the Marketplace. He must be willing to allow her to live as she has lived her entire life—as a freethinking woman, and as an Owner in her own right. And I think it would not be amiss if he were a Master-Trainer. Having a training house in Waterton would be an asset."

Thomas caught his breath. "Me, sir? My lady?" He looked at Lady Margaret, who was nodding. He looked back at Stafford, who smiled.

"A bit of a shock, I'm afraid," Stafford said. "I imagine you thought you would remain a trainer here? Understandable, and this is a fine House with a great tradition. However, you suit my plans nicely, lad. What would you say to a lifetime contract?" He held up his hand to silence Thomas and continued, "I want you to know everything before you answer. You will, to the public, be my Ginny's husband, and the next Baron Waterton. There may be some who say you married beneath your station, but as the youngest son of an impoverished estate, I doubt that. Behind closed doors, however, you will be... well, as you are now. Collared, and owned. What say you?"

Thomas swallowed and looked down at his hands for a moment, feeling the weight of his collar more keenly than he had since it was first locked around his throat. Everything he'd ever dreamed—he looked up sharply. "What does the lady say?" he asked. "Your daughter, is she amenable to this? To being married to one of her slaves?"

His answer was a silvery laugh from behind him, and he turned to see a young woman with hair the color of sunlight through honey standing in the open doors that led out into the gardens. "I do like this one, Papa. Out of all of the ones we've seen, he's the first to ask that," she said, laying an armful of flowers down on the table and coming further into the room. She stopped next to Thomas' chair and smiled down at him. "What is your name?"

Thomas stared up at her for a moment, caught by the golden flecks in her hazel eyes. He heard Lady Margaret's light cough, realized he was staring, and quickly looked down at the Turkish carpet. "Thomas, if it pleases my lady," he answered.

"Well, Thomas, my father has given me final say over this decision. So come with me. We will walk in the garden. It's lovely outside this morning, and I should like to explore the maze."

Thomas rose to his feet and clasped his hands behind his back, fully expecting Lady Margaret and Baron Waterton to join them. When neither of them moved, he hesitated. Surely he wasn't being sent off to walk with Eugenia in the gardens—in the maze!— without a chaperone?

"Thomas," Eugenia said his name, her voice sharp. Thomas snapped to attention and faced her, his eyes lowered so that all he saw was the hem of her dove-gray gown.

"Your cravat, if you please," she said, in a tone that Thomas recognized immediately as *You've made a grave mistake, boy, and you shall pay for it.* He reacted automatically, his hands moving before he truly realized what it was that she'd asked for, and as he unwound the long length of silk from around his throat, he wondered what she was going to do with it. And how he could make amends. He sank to his knees and looked up at her, offering the cravat to her without a word; she took it with a smile and a dimple, unfurling the length of silk that was almost as long as she was tall. Then she said, "Now, Thomas. Bend over. Forehead on the floor, and hands behind your back."

How could one little slip of a girl, one who looked barely old enough to be out of short frocks, have so much control over someone she'd only just met? Thomas wondered as his forehead brushed against the Turkish carpet, wool scratching against his skin as he crossed his wrists behind his back. He heard that silvery laugh again, then felt the soft slither of silk, still warm from his own body, slowly twining around his wrists and binding them fast. She had a talent for it—when she was done and had ordered Thomas back to his feet, he could no more have moved his hands than he could have flown to the moon. Or dreamed of disobeying the devious angel who stood before him, smiling up at him and smoothing the rumpled front of his coat.

"There now," she murmured. "Now Papa and Lady Margaret can have a nice visit, and we can have a lovely walk in the gardens. Come along, Thomas." She turned and walked out the garden door. Without hesitation, Thomas followed her.

They fell into an easy walk once they reached the rose garden, with Thomas a half step behind Eugenia, listening attentively in case she said anything.

"Tell me about yourself, Thomas," she said at last. It wasn't the question Thomas was expecting.

"What would my lady like to know?" he asked.

"Whatever isn't in your file," she answered, smiling at him over her shoulder. "For example, how is it that your family has managed to hide that you are a slave?"

Thomas nodded. "My brother spreads rumors. I'm the family intellectual, according to the common gossip. Lady Margaret is my godmother, and she supports me in my... well, I can't really call them studies. Meanderings, I think, would be a better word. This season, I'm supposed to be somewhere in Egypt. Unwrapping mummies and desecrating tombs, if I remember correctly."

"And your plans, for when you'd finished your training?" she asked.

"In all honesty, my lady, I had thought I would remain here," Thomas said. "I've no desire to give up my collar, and the butler, Mister Bennett, will be retiring after Christmas. I thought I would step into his place, to serve as Lady Margaret's butler and as an under-trainer in her House."

"I think that before then, you'll be mine," Eugenia said. She stopped in one of the conversation nooks located throughout the maze, sitting down on the little bench. Thomas immediately sank to his knees in front of her, forcing himself to ignore the sharp flints that made up the pathway and that were digging into his knees. "You're very attractive, Thomas," Eugenia said, her voice low. "Have you been trained to please in the bedroom?"

Thomas felt his face grow warm, and he looked down. "I've served Lady Margaret and her guests in that capacity, my lady," he murmured. "If you wish to know of my... aptitude, you will have to ask her."

He heard the sound of fabric crinkling and sliding over flesh just before Eugenia said, "I prefer to find some things out for myself." Startled, Thomas looked up to see Eugenia smiling at him, her skirts pulled up to reveal white silk stockings, pale thighs, and sunlight-through-honey curls.

"My lady," Thomas murmured.

"Did I shock you?" Eugenia asked, laughing. "My dear, I'm amused that you've maintained the slightest ability to be shocked, after seven years in a collar. I desire to know if the property I am considering suits me. In all manners."

Thomas looked up and met her eyes. "You have not yet told me what you wish. I would not dare presume—"

"Oh, please presume," Eugenia interrupted. "I'll enjoy correcting you when you've need of it."

Thomas shivered, imagining what punishment at her hands might be like. She looked so delicate, but he knew it was the delicate ones that ofttimes wielded the harshest whip. He leaned forward, gently pressing a kiss to the inside of her right thigh, just over the top of her stocking; she sighed, and he took that as permission to continue, kissing his way up her leg until he reached the juncture of her thighs. He paused, smelling her arousal clearly, knowing that what he did now might change his world forever.

"You may," she purred.

"Thank you, Mistress," Thomas answered. He closed his eyes and pressed a kiss to her curls before dipping lower, delicately flicking his tongue over her pearl. She moaned softly, running her fingers through his hair, and he pressed closer, suckling gently until she gasped and her hips bucked. Would she want him to draw this out? He had no way of knowing. Probably not, since her father and his Trainer were waiting for them. Thomas ran his tongue down between her nether lips, nudging at her clit with his nose while he delved into her quim and tasted her sweetness. She moaned harder, tugging on his hair as he nibbled and licked, flicked and nudged, until at last she crested, muffling her cries of pleasure in her hand.

Thomas drew back, licking his lips and tasting Eugenia's juices like fine wine. Her breathing slowed, and she opened her eyes to look at him; Thomas closed his eyes in pleasure as Eugenia stroked his cheek. He was completely unprepared when she hit him, hard enough to knock him off balance. He landed hard, rolling onto his back, gasping as the stones dug into his bound hands. He looked up to see Eugenia standing over him; she cocked her head to one side, and delicately rested one foot over the tent in Thomas' trousers. As the pressure on his cock slowly increased, Thomas closed his eyes and whimpered, trying to stay still.

"You do very well with pleasuring a woman, Thomas," Eugenia said. "I'm quite pleased. I cannot wait to see what else you know how to do. But that will be later, after we're wed," Eugenia said, pressing a little harder. Thomas' breath quickened, and he bit down on a moan. "You're so fair, you must mark beautifully. I look forward to seeing every bit of you covered in stripes. That will be my gift to you, on our wedding night."

Her foot moved away, and Thomas drew a long, shuddering breath before murmuring, "Thank you, Mistress. If I may be so bold?"

Eugenia laughed. "I appreciate boldness. Go ahead, Thomas."

"My lady will have already given me a gift for our wedding

night," Thomas said as he looked up at her. "My lady will have given me her collar. There is nothing else that may compare to that."

Eugenia caught her breath, and her cheeks flushed slightly. One hand rose, and she touched her lips with the tips of her fingers as she looked at Thomas. After a moment, she smiled prettily and nodded. "Do you need help to get up, Thomas?" she asked.

"No, thank you, my lady," Thomas answered. He didn't move—asking if he needed help getting off the ground was not an invitation to do so.

"Then please stand, Thomas," Eugenia ordered. "We should go back. I will want to be there for the discussion about your contract."

Thomas rolled onto his side, and managed to get onto his knees without doing too much damage to himself or his clothing. Eugenia didn't offer to help, or to free his wrists, and when he reached his feet, she was already walking back to the house. She led the way back into the parlor, and Thomas heard her raised voice as he followed her inside.

"Papa, I'll have Thomas and no other," she announced as she took the chair. Thomas moved into the space next to her and sank to his knees.

"Well, I can see that you've certainly made an impression, my dear," Lady Margaret said, sounding impressed. "Very well, what terms were you thinking?"

Thomas let the conversation move around him without registering what they were speaking of, aware only of Eugenia next to him, of the way she idly started to stroke his hair, as if he were a lap dog or a cat. The contract negotiations were no more than a soft buzzing in his ears, until someone snapped their fingers underneath his nose; he jumped, startled, and heard Eugenia laugh.

"When you're mine, my dear, I'll expect you to pay more mind. Or did you not hear Lady Margaret call your name?"

Thomas felt his face grow hot, and he bent at the waist until his forehead was once again brushing the floor. "I apologize, my ladies, my lord. That was an unforgivable lapse."

Laughter rang out over him, and a light hand ran down the length of his spine; he shuddered and bit his lip.

"Well, I must say, I've never seen my Thomas quite so undone," Lady Margaret said, her amusement clear. "Eugenia, you're going to enjoy him a great deal."

"Thank you, Lady Margaret," Eugenia answered. "I know I shall. Now, if he is supposed to be in Cairo, how shall we arrange this?"

❧

When the planning was done, they all agreed that the match would be the talk of the town—how James Stafford, Baron Waterton, and his daughter, while traveling in Cairo, would attend a lecture where they would meet the Lady Margaret Harrington and her god-son, Thomas Carruthers. It would be love at first sight for Thomas Carruthers and Eugenia Stafford, and the society matrons would sigh for years over the tales of the romantic, whirlwind courtship in exotic lands, culminating in a lavish, high-society wedding when the pair returned to London.

It would have been a marvelous story, if it had actually happened that way.

❧

"Mister Carey, the Lady wishes to see you in her sitting room," one of the maids said, bobbing a slight curtsey. Thomas thanked the girl and started immediately up the stairs, silently giving thanks for the respite from the chaos of arranging to close the house while Lady Margaret traveled abroad. Since this entire trip was for his benefit, Lady Margaret had ordered him to make all of the arrangements for the house and the servants, while she handled the travel arrangements personally. They were due to leave in two days, and she had not yet told Thomas about any of her plans, leaving him mystified as to how they were traveling, or what they were going to do to hide his identity while they were en route.

The sitting room door was ajar, swinging open as Thomas knocked. Inside, Lady Margaret smiled and waved at a large, unfamiliar steamer trunk. "This arrived. Just in time! I had it specially made. There is a company that works with Marketplace owners who have need of discretion, and they've even provided me with the paperwork to avoid having customs examine the interior." She looked very proud of herself, and Thomas smiled as he walked around the trunk. It was far larger than anything that Lady Margaret owned, and he wondered why she needed a new trunk, when her old one was not only in excellent condition, but was already packed.

"It's very nice," he said. In truth, it was. Dark wood polished to a high gloss, shiny brass fittings and heavy leather strappings, and a sturdy lock. The craftsmanship was exquisite. But what was it for?

"Open it," she told him. Puzzled, Thomas unfastened the hasp and opened the trunk; his jaw dropped as he stared at the interior. It was beautifully upholstered inside, with oddly curved and padded wooden shelves. It was, Thomas realized, just big enough inside for a man.

For him.

"My lady!" he sputtered, looking from the padded inside of the trunk to Lady Margaret. "Forgive me, but... you can't mean... this... you want me... in there?"

"Not for the entire journey, my dear," Lady Margaret clarified. "You'll be able to come out when we're on board ship, and once we get to Cairo. Thomas, for this little masquerade to succeed, you cannot be seen with me outside of Cairo. This will keep you hidden away. There are ventilation holes throughout, and you'll be quite safe." She rested one hand on the polished wood case. "I had it made to your measurements. Your own trunks have been packed and sent on ahead, and will meet us in Cairo."

Thomas nodded, struck dumb. He stepped in close and went to one knee, to better examine the interior of the case. He would be sitting, that much was obvious—there was a small wooden shelf at just the right height. Mentally, he overlaid his body with the inside of the case, with the arrangement of shelves, and realized that the oddly curved shelves weren't shelves at all.

"Stocks. Those... those are stocks. I'm going to be locked in the case while bound?" he asked, sounding much more calm than he was feeling. Every story he'd ever heard about shipwrecks were suddenly very clear in his mind.

"For your own protection, my dear. If the case is tipped, or, God forbid, dropped. We don't want you bouncing around on the inside, breaking bones," Lady Margaret explained, resting her hand on his shoulder. "Come, then. Try it on."

Try it on? Thomas silently repeated. He licked his lips and nodded, then looked up. "Is there... a special way? Or do I just climb in?"

Lady Margaret smiled. "You'll need to strip."

Naked, wearing only his locked collar, Thomas followed Lady Margaret's instruction, settling into the wooden seat, positioning his left ankle in the hollow of one of the curved shelves, and watching, intrigued despite his fear, as another curved piece of wood was fit snugly into place with pegs and slots, trapping his left leg and leaving a hollow for his right, a hollow that would be sealed once the case was closed. A similar arrangement, vertical instead of horizontal, was positioned in front of him, ready to trap his wrists and his forearms. More padded stocks pinioned his neck and his waist, and when Lady Margaret closed the case, Thomas found himself completely immobilized, and very aroused.

"Lady Margaret?" he called. "How... how long will I have to be in this?"

The case slid open, and she bent and looked in at him. "You'll be locked away from the time we leave the house until we're safe on board. While we're en route, you'll only need to be secured when I'm not in the stateroom, or if I need to entertain. I cannot carry clothes for you, you understand. Once we reach Port Said, you'll need to be inside the case from when we leave the ship until we reach the hotel in Cairo. That will be the longest part of it, I'm afraid."

"How long?" Thomas repeated. He'd read the guidebooks, but at that moment, he couldn't remember anything but those shipwreck stories.

"According to the information I've been given, you will be encased for twelve hours or more. It will be quite grueling, I should think. But I'm also quite confident in your ability to stay the course. If you think you'll be up for the journey?"

Thomas licked his lips and tried to smile, thinking of the collar he'd have at the end of this and the woman who would put it around his throat. "I'll be fine. This is actually rather comfortable."

"I'm glad you think so. There is one other thing." Lady Margaret turned away, coming back with something in her hands. "We cannot risk you giving yourself away," she said, and showed Thomas the gag she was carrying. "Tonight, you will spend your last night at the foot of my bed. Tomorrow morning, you will be gagged and sealed in the case until we reach the ship," she said firmly. Half-secured in the case, Thomas responded the only way he could—he bowed his head to his Trainer's will.

It was a very good thing that the case was comfortable; since leaving the steam-ship in Port Said, the handling of the case had been very rough, enough that Thomas was very grateful for the padding on the stocks. He took a long breath through his nose and blinked sweat out of his eyes, feeling the lock on his collar bumping against his chest as the case was jostled once more. It was hot in his traveling compartment, the side his left shoulder pressed against growing warmer with each passing moment. They'd none of them thought of how the hotter temperatures in Egypt would affect the insides of the dark traveling case. How long, he wondered, would he be able to remain like this, in this heat, without water? Absently, he tugged on the stocks holding his wrists, already knowing that there would be no slack, no freedom for him until Lady Margaret unlocked the case and released him. So he closed his eyes and forced himself to relax and listen.

Outside, Lady Margaret was scolding the stevedores. Muffled as her voice was by padding and wood, she sounded like a finch; Thomas huffed his amusement and tried to decide if he was going to tell her that or not. He'd just decided not when the case jolted, landing hard on some solid surface. Thomas grunted as the impact rattled his bones, and almost missed Lady Margaret's shrill cries of alarm. The case jolted again, this time tipping over and landing on its side, and Thomas heard shouting before something cut off the tiny pinpoints of light that shone through some ventilation holes, throwing the inside of the case into darkness. There was another lurch, and the case started bumping and rattling violently. It didn't take Thomas long to realize what had happened.

Someone had stolen the case!

Thomas moaned, tugging hard on the stocks. What would happen when they opened the case and discovered that there was nothing of value inside except for him? What would they do to him? Ransom, no doubt. That was, if they believed that the naked man they found bound in a box was really the brother of the Earl of Dunwich. But any ransom demands would ruin his brother. No, he couldn't reveal his real name. He would be Thomas Carey, no more.

More lurid stories came to mind, of white slavers, until Thomas cursed himself for a fool—what did a slave have to fear from slavery? But Lady Margaret? What of her? And Eugenia... she was waiting for him. He tugged hard again on the stocks, trying to shout, trying to be heard outside the case. But no one heard him, and there was nothing he could do as he was spirited away.

It was impossible to gauge how long it had been. Long enough for the air inside the case to grow stuffy from having many of the ventilation holes covered. It was also uncomfortably hot, and Thomas had long since fallen limp, heedless of the pain all along his left side where the hard edges of the stocks were digging into his flesh. His wrists burned and stung, and he knew he must have rubbed them raw trying to pull free when panic took over, sending him into mindless spasms of struggling and muffled screaming, certain that he was never going to see Lady Margaret or Eugenia again.

The rattling and jolting stopped, and Thomas felt the case being moved. He didn't stir, even when the case was raised to its proper position, even when he heard the sounds of the lock being forced. The air rushing into the case as the door swung open felt uncomfortably cold against his skin, and he started to shiver uncontrollably as stocks opened, freeing his right arm and leg, his body, and his throat. His last awareness as he slid from the case and into unconsciousness was of voices he didn't understand crying out in surprise.

He woke when someone dowsed him with water, to find himself lying on a cold dirt floor, his wrists lashed together behind him, the gag gone from his mouth. A man stood over him with an empty bucket and demanded something in Arabic.

"I don't understand you," Thomas said softly. He slowly rolled and got onto his knees, keeping his eyes down and stopping himself from shaking his head to get wet hair out of his eyes. The man snapped something else, but Thomas could only shake his head. Hesitantly, he tried speaking French to his captor, then German, languages the guidebooks said were common in Egypt. Despite the assurances of the guidebooks, this man had neither language, and finally stalked away in disgust, slamming a door behind him. Once the door was closed, Thomas looked around— he was being held in a small, dirty room with no windows and no furnishings, and only a single oil lamp hanging from the ceiling for light. His wrists ached, and he was fiercely thirsty and hungry. He tried to get to his feet, but found that his left ankle was swollen, and would not bear his weight. A few minutes later, another man appeared in the doorway. He looked around, pointed at Thomas, and snapped in broken, heavily accented English, "Who are you?"

"Carey. My name is Thomas Carey," Thomas answered, shifting back onto his knees.

"Why are you in that box? Where the money? Woman said there was... valuable. Gold. Where?"

Thomas shook his head. "No money. No gold. Just me," he said slowly.

"Lies!"

"No!" Thomas insisted. "There's nothing else. Send to my lady. She'll pay to have me back safely. Whatever you want."

The man scowled. "What lady?"

"Lady Margaret Harrington. If she's left Port Said, then she's staying at the Continental Hotel in Cairo," Thomas said. "Send to her. She'll pay you."

The man sniffed and left without another word. The door closed, and Thomas let out a shaky breath, sitting back down in the corner. Lady Margaret wouldn't have left Port Said without him, he was certain. But whom could she contact for help? Thomas remembered her saying that the company that made the case also provided her with paperwork to avoid customs. If she went to the authorities, she would have to tell them what was in the case. Was there a Marketplace liaison in Port Said? Thomas didn't know.

Hours passed, and the light from the lamp slowly started to dim as the oil ran out. Left alone, Thomas dozed in his corner, exhaustion finally defeating hunger, pain and fear. His dreams were filled with vague threats and phantom fears, until he was startled awake by the sound of the door slamming open. In the scant light, he saw stalking towards him the man who had spoken to him in English before, and who looked furious.

"You lie!" he spat, grabbing Thomas by the collar and pulling him to his knees. "No Harrington woman in Port Said!"

Thomas gasped as his collar tightened around his throat. "Didn't... didn't lie..." he forced out.

The man scoffed and backhanded Thomas across the face. "Lies. Madman. You are a danger to all of us!" He hit Thomas again, this time letting him fall the floor before dragging him back to his knees by the hair.

"Now, you tell me, mad Englishman. Why we keep you alive?" a voice growled into his ear. Thomas shuddered, and realized that he had one bargaining chip. He stopped struggling and forced himself to go limp, leaning back against his captor.

"I can show you a reason," he murmured, keeping his voice low. "May I show you?"

He heard something guttural over his head—a curse?—and then he was pushed forward. Not hard enough to throw him on the ground, but hard enough that he had to struggle to keep to his knees. He turned and looked over his shoulder, to see the other man studying him.

"You show," he declared.

Thomas ducked his head and crawled towards him, keeping his eyes on his captor's feet. When he was close enough, he raised his head and leaned forward, breathing on the other man's crotch before he started to rub his cheek against the man's flaccid cock. He alternated nuzzling and breathing, and as the tent started to grow, he started mouthing the other man's cock through the rough woven fabric. Above him, Thomas could hear short gasping breaths, and the hint of a moan. Then he was pushed back, and told, "Wait. You wait."

Thomas sat back on his heels and waited as the other man left the room, coming back with several cushions that he tossed on the floor in the corner. Then he stripped off his trousers and sat down, leaning against the cushions, his erection standing upright like a pole. He waved at Thomas. "Now, you finish."

Thomas licked his lips and considered, then nodded and crawled forward, folding at the waist, opening his mouth and swallowing the other man's cock whole, then raised himself up and started running his tongue around the swollen head. Fingers tightened in his hair, and Thomas found his head being shoved down hard, pulled back, then shoved down even harder, until his face was pressed up against his captor's belly, and he could no longer breathe past the cock in his throat. He struggled, trying to push himself up, but the hand didn't relent; Thomas heard laughter, His head was pulled back up, and he gasped for air before being brutally pushed back down.

It went on like this for what felt like a very long time, until Thomas thought he was going to swoon from lack of air. Until at last the man growled and spent, shooting his seed down Thomas' throat, and laughing uproariously as Thomas gagged and spat, then gagged again. He pushed Thomas away and rose, pulling his trousers back on. Once he was again dressed, he used one foot to push Thomas onto his back.

"Harrington, you say? At Continental?" he asked.

"Yes," Thomas said, licking his swollen lips. He rolled onto his side, and slowly got back to his knees, bowing his head slightly.

"Cairo," the man said. "I send one man. If he does not come back, you die. And until then, you slave." He shoved Thomas back to the floor, looked down at him and smiled, the sight enough to make Thomas shudder. Then he stalked out, and the door closed behind him. Thomas sighed, swallowing and feeling the ache in his throat. Hopefully, he wouldn't have to do it again.

A few minutes later, the door opened. Thomas froze, but it was a young man, a stranger, who came inside carrying a bowl in one hand, a battered tin cup in the other, and a bundle under his arm. He came over to Thomas and sat down on the floor, helping Thomas to sit and holding the cup under his nose.

"Drink," he said. Thomas nodded; the water was brackish, but Thomas was too thirsty to care. When it was empty, the cup was set aside, and the young man held up the bowl, "Bomani say to eat."

"Thank you," Thomas said. He looked at the bowl and then at the young man, who smiled and started to feed him. Thomas nodded his thanks, chewing slowly and studying the young man in front of him with the practiced eye of a Trainer. No more than twenty, surely, and a startlingly beautiful youth, he was as out of place among the rough kidnappers as a pearl among stones. What was he doing here? Thomas wondered, and nodded towards the door. "He is Bomani?"

The young man nodded. "Bomani. Yes."

"And you are?" Thomas asked. The man frowned, and Thomas nodded towards him. "You. Your name?"

"Ah. Ishaq. Ishaq, me." Ishaq smiled again and fed Thomas another bite. They didn't speak again until Thomas was done. Then Ishaq frowned, touching Thomas' collar.

"You..." he frowned again, obviously looking for the word. Then he nodded. "Marketplace? You slave?"

"You know?" Thomas blurted out, too shocked to think of anything else to say. Ishaq laughed.

"Yes. I..." he frowned again, and then shook his head. "Not... words. I... help?"

Thomas caught his breath and looked past Ishaq to the partially open door. Then he looked back at Ishaq and whispered in French, "Do you understand me?"

Ishaq's eyes widened, and he nodded before answering in the same language, "Yes."

"How do you know the Marketplace?" Thomas asked.

"Bomani... he and his men waylaid my brothers and I, when we were en route to bring me to my trainer. We had no money to give him, so he murdered my brothers, and he kept me... the way he keeps you. The way he will keep you." Ishaq looked over his shoulder and pitched his voice lower. "He's already calling you his English whore."

Thomas shivered. "Better to kill me."

"When he gets bored of you, he will," Ishaq murmured. Thomas frowned, and then realized what Ishaq wasn't saying.

"He's going to kill you?" he whispered.

Ishaq nodded. "Tonight. Tomorrow. Soon," he said. "Unless... tell me. Your master was where?"

"Lady Margaret Harrington. If she went to Cairo, she would be at the Continental Hotel. But I don't think she left Port Said."

Ishaq nodded. "I can get to Port Said. I... the night guard, he wants me. Before, he would not, because Bomani would have killed him. Now, Bomani has you, and he no longer cares for me. I can seduce the night guard, get out of here."

"And if they find you, they'll kill you!" Thomas hissed.

"I am already dead!" Ishaq insisted. "But this way... it is better." He smiled and reached out to touch the lock on Thomas' collar. He fell silent, cleaning up the bowl and cup, and then unrolled the bundle to reveal a ragged blanket. He wrapped it around Thomas' shoulders and helped him to lie down, sitting next to him for a several minutes without a word. Thomas found his presence oddly comforting, closing his eyes and trying not to think too much about what was at risk. This beautiful boy... was he really going to risk his life for Thomas? What would happen if he failed? Thomas tried very hard not to think of that possibility. Eventually, he slipped into a fitful sleep. Thankfully, he did not dream.

Thomas woke to the sounds of shouting, and Bomani bursting into the room, his voice angry as he railed at Thomas in Arabic. Blinking away sleep, Thomas struggled free of the blanket and sat up, only to be knocked back to the floor with a blow from one of Bomani's fists, and then kicked hard enough that he felt his body rise up off the floor. Thomas lay still, moaning in pain, until Bomani grabbed him by the collar, pulling him to his knees and holding him there, struggling for breath as Bomani slapped him once more.

"Where is he?" Bomani finally demanded in English. "Ishaq? Where is he?" He slapped Thomas again, shaking him hard before dropping him back onto the floor.

Thomas gasped for breath, curling into a ball to protect himself from any other kicks, and finally managing to stammer, "Don't...

don't know!"

"Liar," Bomani snapped, his foot catching Thomas' left ankle, making Thomas howl in pain. "Where is he?"

"I don't know!" Thomas insisted, panting. "Please, I don't know where he's gone."

"You tell me!" Bomani said. He left the room for a moment, then came back in carrying something that Thomas recognized immediately: a singlestick. Bomani laughed as he tapped the wooden cudgel against his palm. "You tell me," he repeated.

The beating went on long after Thomas' protests of ignorance turned into screams of pain, begging and tears, lasting until the singlestick snapped in two. Thomas was barely conscious at that point, only able to whimper feebly as Bomani grabbed him, his fingers digging into Thomas' hips as he was pulled onto his knees and his legs pushed apart. Thomas closed his eyes as Bomani's cock shoved hard against his ass—he'd known this was coming, expected it. That didn't change the fact that the pain was more shrill than any that Thomas had ever experienced; his tortured voice couldn't produce anything more than a strangled whimper, which only seemed to act as a goad for Bomani's brutal pleasure. Bomani growled over him, slamming hard against him until Thomas was sure that he was going to be ripped in two.

Bomani spent quickly, pulling out hard and kicking Thomas again as he rose; Thomas lay where he fell and didn't move, didn't even bother opening his eyes when he heard the sharp snap of a gun cocking. Gunfire roared, loud enough that Thomas' ears rang. He opened his eyes to see Bomani dead! His chest was a red ruin, and beyond him, in the doorway, stood a strange, dark skinned man, well-dressed and carrying a hunting rifle. His mouth moved, but Thomas heard not a word as his world went black.

* * *

When Thomas woke, he was in a bed, surrounded by white gauze curtains. He was clean, wearing a light nightshirt, and his collar was gone. Both of his wrists were bandaged, and Thomas could feel tight strapping around his ribs, and around his left ankle. Slowly, he sat up and pulled back the bed-curtains so that he could look around, wincing as the movement set off a cacophony of aches and pains. The room was neat and sparsely furnished, with high, wide windows and high ceilings. Where was he?

He didn't have to wait long for an answer—there was a knock at the door, and an older man with skin the colored of polished mahogany entered, followed by a younger woman carrying a tray. The man looked at him and smiled, and Thomas recognized him as the man who had killed Bomani.

"Well, how do you feel, Thomas?" he asked.

"Very well, thank you," Thomas answered slowly. He watched as the woman came closer, setting the tray on the edge of the bed; a collar was visible over the edge of her long tunic. She didn't meet his eyes, hurrying out of the room as silently as she'd entered. Thomas looked back at the man and bowed his head, "Thank you, sir."

The man laughed, "I am Nizam. I am the Master Trainer for Lower Egypt. And you... you, my friend, are very lucky. We have been hunting those marauders for months. They preyed on travelers, and always managed to vanish into the desert without a trace. Those we took alive will be tried and probably executed for their crimes."

Thomas nodded, ignoring the tray. "And Ishaq? He's safe?"

"Safe and well. You have no idea how surprised I was, to see again after half a year the young man who was supposed to start his training in this house, and who we'd given up for dead!" Nizam said. "He says that it is your doing that he was able to escape them."

"I... distracted their leader," Thomas said softly. Nizam grunted, his expression serious.

"I saw what distraction you mean, Thomas," he said. "My physician has assured me that you took no lasting damage from the beating, or what followed. Your ankle is damaged, though. If you listen, and if you do as you are told, you will probably not have too much of a limp." Nizam smiled broadly. "And it is something you do well, I think. To listen, and do as you are told."

Thomas smiled and ducked his head. "As my lord says," he murmured, drawing a laugh from the other man.

"Now, you will eat, and rest. Your lady was here—"

"Lady Margaret?" Thomas interrupted. Nizam raised his eyebrows in exaggerated surprise, and Thomas felt his face grow warm. "I apologize, sir," he said quietly.

"As I was saying," Nizam said. "Lady Margaret was a guest in my house, until this morning when she boarded the train for Cairo. She said to tell you that you are an exasperating man, that if you hadn't already been beaten far worse than she could ever manage, that she would punish you for getting kidnapped, and that she will be coming back with your new Owner. She will return in two or three days. And she says that while you are convalescing, you should consider yourself released from her collar."

Thomas reached up and touched his naked throat. "She didn't have to do that," he murmured.

"No, she did not," Nizam agreed. "But she said you need to heal, and decide. And that some decisions are best made as a free man, and not as a slave. As it happens, I agree with her. You are my welcome guest, Thomas Carruthers."

Thomas rubbed his fingers over his collarbone, then murmured, "Thank you, sir. Ah... is Ishaq at other duties? Might I see him?"

Nizam laughed again. "That one!" he said. "Every time he has been given permission to ask a question, he asks for you. I will send him, so that you might each be assured the other is whole."

Nizam left, and Thomas turned his attention to the tray, eating slowly, savoring each bite. He was almost finished when he heard the door open. He looked up, and almost didn't recognize Ishaq, dressed neatly in a long blue tunic and white trousers, and with a collar shining against his dusky skin. Thomas smiled broadly.

"Ishaq!" he called in French. "Come in! Please, I have so much for which to thank you..." His voice trailed off as Ishaq went to his knees and bowed his head.

"I should be thanking you, sir," he said softly. "I am thanking you. I have been told that whatever you request, whatever you desire of me, I may give to you. How may I serve, sir?"

It took Thomas a moment to find his voice, and when he did, it shook as he spoke. "Ishaq, I have no desires, save only that I don't wish formal manners from you."

Ishaq relaxed slightly. "Thank you, sir," he said. "I was... nervous. Master says you are a trainer! And that you are no longer a slave. I was not certain how to approach you."

"I am a slave between owners," Thomas answered. "Now, come up here and let me look at you." He smiled as Ishaq rose and come over to the bed. "You look good. They didn't hurt you, did they?"

Ishaq shook his head. "No, Thomas. The night guard... he was nothing compared to Bomani. He was easy to deal with, and I was away before the moon rose. Master... told me that you had been hurt...?"

"I'll be fine, Ishaq," Thomas said. "I chose that route, and it saved both our lives." He looked around, eager to change the subject. "Where are we, Ishaq?"

"Port Said," Ishaq answered. "Master has something to do with the canal. Shipping, I think. I do not understand it. He says I will learn. Would you like me to take your tray?"

"Please!" Thomas answered. "I feel like the Christmas goose, I'm that full. And I don't even know what it was that I ate!"

Ishaq smiled and took the tray out of the room, returning a moment later and coming over to stand by the bedside. "Thomas... what may I do for you?"

It took Thomas a moment to realize what Ishaq was asking, and he smiled and gestured for the slave to sit. "Ishaq, anything you could do to or for me right now, I'm in no condition to appreciate, let alone enjoy. Your company is all I'd like."

Ishaq nodded once, his expression grave. "Then I will keep you company. Master says that you are now my only responsibility, Thomas."

They talked for hours, with Ishaq describing the scenes outside the window, telling Thomas about Port Said, and about his hopes to see Cairo. He told Thomas about his childhood in Qatia, a town east of the canal. In return, Thomas told Ishaq about England, about his time in service, and about Eugenia. They shared another meal, and as the dusk started to cast long shadows on the floor, Thomas leaned back against his pillows and sighed.

"I thought I'd never see her again," he said. "She's... Ishaq, she's every dream I ever had, made flesh. She'll be my wife, and my Mistress, and my owner, for the rest of my life." He didn't say the thought that haunted him—that she might no longer want him.

"And she's coming here, for you," Ishaq said. "Perhaps, someday, I might be as lucky?"

Thomas looked at him and smiled. "Perhaps yes. You deserve it. I'm tired, Ishaq."

"Sleep, Thomas," Ishaq said softly. He rose and pulled the sheets up to cover Thomas to the chest. "She'll be here soon, my friend. Sleep."

জ্ড

Thomas slept most of the second day, waking only for meals. On the morning of the third day, he was seen by Nizam's physician, who pronounced him hale, allowed him to dress and ordered him to stay off his ankle. Ensconced in a chair by the windows, Thomas was fretting before midday, unused to enforced idleness.

"Ishaq, there has to be something I can do!" he exclaimed as Ishaq came into the room. "Is there anything? Would you ask Nizam?"

"There are books you could read," Ishaq answered. "If you wish to write letters, I will bring a writing desk. If you wish to play chess, or cards, I will find someone to play, because I do not know how to play yet. I can teach you how to play senet. Or I can take you back to bed. That is all my Master has said you are allowed to do." Ishaq answered, a small smile on his face.

Thomas grumbled, then sighed. "Bring a chessboard and help me to the table. I'll teach you to play."

Teaching Ishaq the intricacies of chess took the better part of the afternoon—the young slave proved to be a quick study, and possessing of a devious mind. Once he understood the basics, playing against him was both enjoyable and unpredictable. Thomas was so engrossed in the game that he didn't hear the door open, didn't notice that anyone else was in the room until Ishaq gasped, jumped to his feet, then dropped to his knees. Thomas looked up, startled, to see Lady Margaret smiling at him.

"My lady!" he gasped. He gripped the arms of his chair, looked down, and then looked back up at her. "Please forgive me. I can't..." his voice trailed off, and he closed his eyes tightly and took a long breath. "I'm sorry!" he gasped, feeling a tightness in his chest that threatened to overwhelm him. He heard a quick rustling, and familiar arms wrapped around him, holding him tight.

"It's over now, my dear," Lady Margaret murmured. "It's over."

Safe in her arms, Thomas cried, hearing her assurances only as comforting noise, until at last he raised his head and wiped his face with one shaking hand.

"I'm sorry," he repeated, his voice harsh. "I've been so much trouble..."

"It was none of it your fault, my dear," Lady Margaret said. "Nizam's physician says that you'll be fine."

Thomas nodded. "He told me this morning. My lady, why did you take my collar?"

Lady Margaret didn't look surprised at the question. She nodded and sat down in Ishaq's abandoned chair. Ishaq, Thomas noticed, had vanished.

"Thomas, Nizam told me what had been done to you, what you had to do to survive. I worried that you might... resent the collar, because of it. I thought that you might better be able to decide what you wanted if you could think on it with all of your choices available. You could remain in service and sign that lifetime contract. You could leave service, and marry Eugenia as a free man and a Trainer. Or you could leave the Marketplace entirely."

Thomas looked out the window, and then looked back at Lady Margaret. "Does she want me still?" he asked.

"Perhaps you should ask me?" a quiet voice asked, and Thomas turned to see Eugenia standing in the doorway, Ishaq behind her. She turned and thanked him, then came further into the room. Without a word, Lady Margaret patted Thomas on the shoulder and left with Ishaq.

Eugenia came forward until her skirts brushed against Thomas' legs. "Do I still want you?" she asked. "Thomas, they told me what happened, what was done to you. They told me... and I think that the better question is do you still want me?"

He looked up into her gold-flecked eyes and told her the complete truth, "With all my heart."

She smiled slightly. "With or without a collar? Before you answer, know that I'll marry you regardless of your choice."

"I would be honored to wear your collar, Mistress," Thomas said softly. To his surprise, Eugenia leaned down and kissed him, then slipped into his lap, curling against his chest.

"My darling," she murmured as he wrapped his arms around her. "I'm tempted to say hang it all to waiting until after the wedding, and take you to bed right here and how. But it would upset Papa."

Thomas smiled, breathing in the scent of the woman in his arms. "We shouldn't upset your father."

"No, we won't," Eugenia agreed, playing with the braid on the front of Thomas' tunic. "And you still need time to heal. We'll have to change the story, you know. You weren't in Cairo, and everyone at the Continental knows we left in a great rush."

Thomas frowned, thinking. Then he laughed.

"I think I know what to say."

❦

The match was the talk of the town—how Thomas Carruthers,

youngest brother of the Earl of Dunwich, was kidnapped by brigands while traveling in Egypt. Upon his rescue, he was attended by his visiting godmother, Lady Margaret Harrington, and her traveling companions, James Stafford, Baron Waterton, and his daughter Eugenia. It was love at first sight for Thomas Carruthers and Eugenia Stafford, and the society matrons sighed for years over the tales of the marriage of the invalid and his loving nurse, casting them as paragons of propriety. That, they said, was how a proper marriage should be!

Behind closed doors, bound and collared to his Mistress' whim, Thomas could only agree.

THE MARKETPLACE SERIES

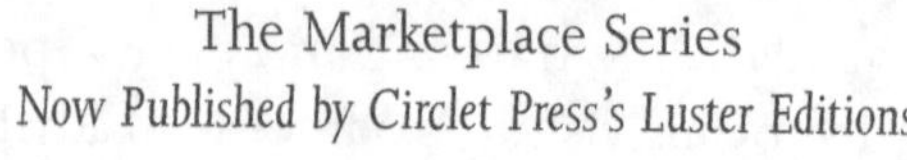

The Marketplace Series
Now Published by Circlet Press's Luster Editions

Circlet Press is proud to be returning the entire *Marketplace* series by Laura Antoniou to print, as well as launching all-new ebook editions. These books are the first in our Luster Editions line of erotic books and books of alternative sexuality that are not science fiction or fantasy.

The Marketplace
  $9.99 ebook, $19.95 paperback
The Slave
  $9.99 ebook, $19.95 paperback
The Trainer
  $9.99 ebook, $19.95 paperback
The Academy
  $9.99 ebook, $19.95 paperback
The Reunion, coming Summer 2013!
The Inheritor—in the works!

Stand-alone short stories also available as downloads for 99 cents each!

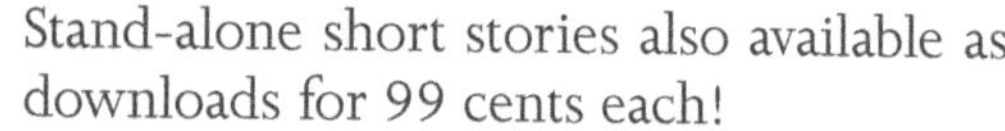

For Want of a Nail
That's Harsh!
California Dreamin'

For More Information
www.circlet.com

THE MARKETPLACE SERIES

"This is the kind of virtual world that has the same enduring appeal as those of the best fantasy novels."—*Erotica Revealed*

"The landmark Marketplace Series… set the standard for contemporary SM erotica. These books chronicle the adventures of those who live in an enticing world built on a slave-based hierarchy, where realistic characters are confronted with questions of trust and duty amidst an ambience of pain and eroticism."
—*The Erotic Lure*

"…Antoniou is a strong writer. Her books have engaging storylines, developed characters, and startlingly realistic descriptions of BDSM relationships. Antoniou's novels represent some of the finest BDSM erotica today."
—*Miss Abernathy's Concise Slave Training Manual*

"With her creation of the fictitious Marketplace, an elite and secretive world organizations, dedicated to the auctioning and overseeing of the world's finest lifestyle slaves, Antoniou has achieved a feat of which few writers are capable: she has constructed a world so vivid in sequel after sequel, it takes on a reality of its own, one that's visually hard to let go of once the reader has put down the book."—*Libido*

The Viscountess Investigates

by Cameron Quintain

$6.99 ebook

Now in paperback! $12.95

The regal Viscountess and her partner Severin are not your typical detectives, nor your typical mistress/slave pair from the BDSM subculture. They inhabit the magical and kinky world hidden by the powerful spell known as the Blindfold, and they travel from the Real World into magical Dominions that reflect every kink fantasy humans can dream of. When the powerful leader of the Algophilia Society is murdered, their path to track down the killer brings them through a Victorian London that never was.

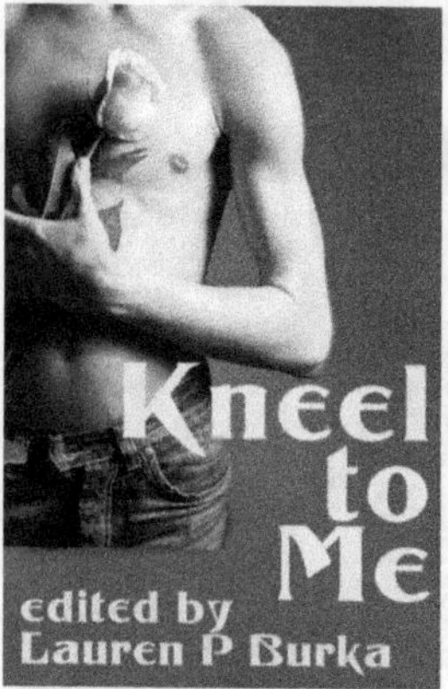

Kneel To Me edited by Lauren P. Burka

ISBN: 978-1-885865-54-0 $6.99

Circlet Press brings you seven erotic stories of dominance and submission that will return you to the moment when a master, mistress, or slave first stepped out of a story and made you theirs.

Like A Thorn: BDSM Fairy Tales

edited by Cecilia Tan & Sarah Desautels

ISBN: 978-1-885865-85-4 $5.99

Five classic fairy tales reemerge as deliciously dark erotica stories with a BDSM twist. You'll discover .how a witch really likes to punish naughty interlopers, why Beauty might love her beast more than the prince, how to produce handy bruises when a pea just won't do the trick– and more. Ranging from present day to "once upon a time" settings, each story offers a fresh perspective to both legend and BDSM.